Christmas 2013
To dear Elizabeth.

D0980188

WANDA E. BRUNSTETTER

BARBOUR
PUBLISHING

© 2012 by Wanda E. Brunstetter

Print ISBN 978-1-61626-661-5

eBook Editions:
Adobe Digital Edition (.epub) 978-1-60742-860-2
Kindle and MobiPocket Edition (.prc) 978-1-60742-861-9

All rights reserved. No part of this publication may be reproduced or transmitted for commercial purposes, except for brief quotations in printed reviews, without written permission of the publisher.

Churches and other noncommercial interests may reproduce portions of this book without the express written permission of Barbour Publishing, provided that the text does not exceed 500 words or 5 percent of the entire book, whichever is less, and that the text is not material quoted from another publisher. When reproducing text from this book, include the following credit line: "From *Double Trouble: What a Pair!*, published by Barbour Publishing, Inc. Used by permission."

All German Dutch words are from the *Revised Pennsylvania Dutch Dictionary* found in Lancaster County, Pennsylvania.

Scripture taken from the HOLY BIBLE, NEW INTERNATIONAL VERSION®. NIV®. Copyright © 1973, 1978, 1984, 2011 by Biblica, Inc.™ Used by permission. All rights reserved worldwide.

This book is a work of fiction. Names, characters, places, and incidents are either products of the author's imagination or used fictitiously. Any similarity to actual people, organizations, and/or events is purely coincidental.

Cover illustration: Colleen Madden/MB Artists

Published by Barbour Publishing, Inc., P.O. Box 719, Uhrichsville, Ohio 44683, www.barbourbooks.com

Our mission is to publish and distribute inspirational products offering exceptional value and biblical encouragement to the masses.

Member of the
Evangelical Christian
Publishers Association

Printed in the United States of America.
Dickinson Press, Inc., Grand Rapids, MI 49512; August 2012; D10003449

DEDICATION

To the children of my Amish friends who live in Ohio, and a special thanks to everyone who shared some of their humorous childhood memories with me.

GLOSSARY

absatz—stop
ach—oh
aldi—girlfriend
appenditlich—delicious
baremlich—terrible
boppli—baby
bruder—brother
buch—book
busslin—kittens
daed—dad
danki—thanks
daremlich—dizzy
dumm—dumb
frosch—frog
grank—sick
hochmut—pride
hund—dog
hundli—puppy
hungerich—hungry
jah—yes
kaes—cheese
kapps—caps
katze—cats

koppweh—headache
kumme—come
mamm—mom
meh—more
melke—milk
narrisch—crazy
oier—eggs
pannekuche—pancakes
pescht—pest
schlang—snake
schmaert—smart
schpass—fun
schtinke—stink
voll schpaas—very funny
windle—diapers
wunderbaar—wonderful

Guder mariye, schlofkopp—Good morning, sleepyhead
Ich verschreck net graad—I don't frighten easily
Is fattgange—Go away

CONTENTS

The Amish are a group of people who, due to their religious beliefs, live a plain life without the use of many modern things. Early Amish people lived in Europe, but many came to America in the 1700s so they could worship freely. More than 250,000 Amish now live in the United States and Canada.

The Old Order Amish wear plain clothes, much like the American pioneers used to wear. For everyday, the women and girls wear plain, solid-colored dresses and small head coverings, or *kapps*, on their heads. Some may wear dark head scarves when they are working around their homes and yards. For church, funerals, weddings, and other special occasions, Amish women and girls wear white aprons over their dresses. Amish men and boys wear plain cotton shirts, trousers with suspenders, and straw hats. For church and other special occasions they wear dark pants with matching jackets and black felt hats.

Because they believe electricity is too modern to have in their homes, Amish people use kerosene, propane gas, coal, diesel fuel, and wood for heating, cooking, and running their machinery and appliances. Telephones are not allowed inside an Old Order Amish home, but some Amish have phones in their shops, barns, or sheds outside the home. Amish people use a horse and buggy when they travel within ten to fifteen miles from their homes, but ride in cars with hired drivers to take them on longer trips where it's too far to drive with their buggies.

At one time, most Amish men farmed for a living, but now many work in various jobs. Some are blacksmiths, harness makers, carpenters, painters, storekeepers, or might work in several other trades. Some Amish women who need to work outside their home earn money by selling eggs, fruits and vegetables, or handmade items such as dolls, quilts, and craft items. Others work in gift shops, bakeries, or restaurants, and some have other occupations as well.

Amish children, called "scholars," usually attend one-room schoolhouses from grades one to eight. Once they finish the eighth grade and leave school, they spend time learning a trade so they can get a job and earn money to support themselves and their families. The children learn three languages: English, German, and Pennsylvania-Dutch, which is the language they usually speak when they are with family and friends. German is spoken when the ministers read the Bible and preach during church services. English is learned when a child attends school in the first grade, and it's spoken when the Amish are with other people who aren't Amish.

The Amish hold their church services every other week, in the home, shop, or barn of different church members. The largest Amish community in the United States is in Holmes County, Ohio, where my story about Amish children, Mark and Mattie Miller, is set.

CHAPTER 1

Flying High

"*Kumme*, Mattie! Let's play a game!" Mattie Miller's eight-year-old twin brother called to her from across the yard.

Looking toward Mark, Mattie shook her head. "I don't want to play a game right now." She'd been lying on a blanket in the grass, looking at the puffy white clouds above, and didn't want to be disturbed.

"Aw, come on, Mattie. It'll be *schpass*!" Mark ran through the grass in his bare feet, kicking up several grasshoppers, and then he plopped down beside her.

"If you think it'll be fun, it probably won't be for me," Mattie mumbled. "Besides, I'm busy right now."

"Busy doing what? You don't look busy to me," he said, removing his straw hat and tossing it on the ground.

Mattie held back a chuckle. When Mark took off his hat his thick red hair stuck straight up. She was glad her hair never did that. Of course, Mattie usually wore her long red hair pulled up in a bun, with a small black cap on top of her head. Sometimes, for playing or doing chores, she would wear a dark-colored scarf, like she had on today.

"Can't you see that I'm watching the clouds?" she asked, once the urge to laugh at Mark's hair had passed.

Mark leaned back on his elbows and looked up at the summer sky. "Know what a cloud's made of?"

"Cotton?"

"No way! Clouds are droplets of water or ice crystals that float high above the earth."

"Is that so?"

"*Jah.*" Mark looked kind of smug as he nodded and said, "Did you know that clouds come in all different sizes and shapes?" He knew a lot about many things, but Mattie knew a few things he didn't know—about flowers, dogs, and the best way to hit a baseball when it was coming toward you really fast.

"There are several types of clouds," Mark went on to say. "There are cirrus, cirrostratus, cirrocumulus, altocumulus, and cumulus clouds."

"Those are all such big words." Mattie frowned. "Can't we just call them clouds?"

"We could, but I thought you'd like to know the names of each type of cloud. Now, cumulus clouds are the most common kind. They're usually fair weather clouds."

"Like we're having today?"

"That's right," Mark said with a nod.

The twins stayed on the grass for a while, watching the clouds drift lazily across the sky.

"Look over there, Mark!" Mattie pointed to a particularly unusual-looking cloud. "That one's shaped like a swan. Isn't it pretty?"

"Uh-huh." Mark didn't look all that impressed, but then what did a boy know about things being pretty?

"Look there." Mattie pointed up and to the right. "That one looks like a big fish."

"I see them both, but they're quickly changing. Now they don't look like a swan or a fish anymore. It must be because of the different air currents movin' them around." Mark nudged Mattie's arm. "Are ya ready to play a game with me now?"

"Oh, all right." Mattie knew if she didn't do what Mark wanted, he'd just keep pestering her until she finally gave in. As much as she loved her twin brother, sometimes—like now—he was so full of energy she couldn't keep up with him.

Mark helped Mattie to her feet, and then he led her into the center of the yard. When he pulled a strip of dark blue material from his pants pocket, Mattie became a bit concerned.

"What's that for?" she asked.

"This is a blindfold, and I'm gonna put it over your eyes. Then I'll tie it around the back of your head."

Mattie shook her head vigorously. "I don't want to be blindfolded! I won't be able to see where I'm going, and I might trip and fall on something."

"There's no need to worry," Mark said with a grin. "I'll look after you, and I'll even hang on to your arm."

Mattie was suspicious about playing this game with Mark. Besides being smart, he was also a big tease and liked to play tricks on her whenever he could. For now, though, she decided to play along with her brother and let him have his fun.

"I don't know about this," Mattie said.

Mark gave her arm a little squeeze. "It'll be okay, I promise."

"Well, okay." Mattie stood patiently as Mark started to put the piece of cloth over her eyes.

"Oops, wait a minute," he said. "You have some grass in your hair. Let me get it off before I put the blindfold on."

Mattie watched as he concentrated on getting all the loose grass out of her hair. In many ways they were alike. When they stood side by side you could see right away that their hair was the exact same color of red, and their blue eyes matched, too. But in many ways they were as different as night and day.

I'm glad I was the one who ended up with a few freckles on my nose, and not ears that stick out a bit the way Mark's do, Mattie thought. She would never tease her twin brother about it, though. It was bad enough that some of the boys they knew sometimes teased him about his ears, as well as being so smart. A few of them made fun of his red hair, too.

"Okay, I've got all the grass out of your hair now," Mark said, as he tied the blindfold behind Mattie's head. "I'm gonna spin you around, and then I'll walk you all around the yard. When we stop, you'll have to speculate where you are."

Mattie tipped her head. "Speculate? What's that?"

"It means 'guess.'"

Mattie was confused. Mark was always using words she didn't understand. Sometimes, when he wouldn't tell her what those big words meant, she had to get a dictionary and look them up so she'd know what he was talking about. "What happens if I guess where I am?" Mattie asked.

"You win the game, plus you get a prize." Mark snickered. "But if you don't know where you are, then I win the game and I get a prize."

"What's the prize?"

"If you win, I'll do one of your chores tonight; and if I win, you'll have to do one of mine."

Mattie wasn't sure she liked this game, but she knew their yard quite well and thought she'd be able to guess where she was with no trouble at all. If she won, it would be nice to have Mark do one of her chores. Maybe she would ask him to wash the dishes. While he was stuck in the kitchen with his hands in soapy water, she'd be in her room playing with her dolls or reading the book about flowers she'd been given for Christmas last year.

"Okay, little *bruder*; spin me around," she finally agreed.

"I am not your little brother, because we were both born at the same time."

"But Mom said I was born ten minutes before you, so that means I'm older and you're my little bruder."

"Whatever!" Mark put his hands on Mattie's shoulders and spun her around several times.

"*Absatz!* Stop! You're making me *daremlich*!"

"You won't be dizzy once we start walking." Mark took hold of Mattie's arm and led her across the lawn. She knew they were still in the yard because she could feel the cold grass tickling her bare toes.

"Is it time for me to guess where I am?" she asked.

"Not yet."

Mark gave Mattie a couple more spins, and then led her off in another direction. She wouldn't admit it to Mark, but she felt mixed up. Mattie hoped he didn't ask her to guess where she was now, because she really wasn't sure.

Suddenly, Mark let go of Mattie's arm. She teetered back and forth, feeling even dizzier than before, and struggling to keep her balance. When the spinning sensation finally stopped, she took a step forward and reached out her hand. "Mark?"

No reply.

"Are you there, Mark? You said you would hold on to my arm, but you're not holding it now. Mark, where are you?"

Still no response.

"Mark, you'd better answer me right now."

Nothing. Not even a peep.

Mattie turned, and with her hands outstretched, she took a few steps in the other direction. "Mark Miller, you'd better not leave me out here like this!"

Tee-hee. She heard Mark snicker from somewhere nearby.

"What's so funny? Where am I, Mark? And where are you?"

"It's okay. You're just a little discombobulated right now."

"Dis-com-what?"

"Discombobulated. It means mixed up, or confused. Now, take three steps forward," Mark said.

Holding her arms straight out, Mattie counted out loud as she began to walk. "One. . .two. . .three. . ."

"That's good. Now turn to the right—no, I mean left. Then take two more steps."

Mattie turned and—*smack!*—bumped into something.

"Ouch! Did I just smack into the barn?"

"Sorry about that," Mark said. "Just take a step back and turn to the right."

Gritting her teeth, Mattie turned in the direction Mark told her to, knowing she definitely did not like this game! She'd only taken a few steps, when something prickly stabbed her knees. "Yeow! What was that?"

Mattie jumped backward and something went—*crunch!* She knew she wasn't on the grass. "Am I in Mom's flower bed?"

Mattie pulled the blindfold off her head and realized that she was in one of Mom's flower beds and had broken off a piece of the rosebush. She saw Mark several feet away, laughing and clutching his stomach.

"It's not funny! I'm done with this silly game!" She started to walk away, but turned back around. "Oh, and I guessed where I was, so you'll have to do the dishes for me tonight."

Mark opened his mouth like he was going to say

something, but just then Mom shouted from the porch, "Mattie Miller, what were you doing in my flower bed? You've ruined some of my beautiful roses!"

Mattie explained about the game she and Mark had been playing, and how he'd let go of her arm. "First I bumped into the barn, and then—sorry, Mom, but I somehow ended up in the flower bed."

"You certainly did." Mom frowned and shook her finger at the twins. "You two had better find another game to play. If you don't, I'll give you both some work to do."

"I'm sorry, Mom, it won't happen again," Mattie said, looking at the flowers she'd ruined.

"Apology accepted. Just please see to it that you and your brother stay out of trouble." Mom started to turn toward the door, but whirled back around. "Oh, I'll be leaving shortly to pick up Perry and Ada at your Grandma and Grandpa Miller's."

"Okay, Mom." No way did Mattie want to make Mom angry or do any extra work, so she went back to her blanket and flopped down to watch the clouds some more. It was one sure way to stay out of mischief— especially with her twin brother!

While Mattie reclined on the grass staring up at the clouds, Mark went to the barn and sat on a bale of straw, trying to think up something else that would be fun to do. It had been funny to see his twin sister blindfolded, stumbling around the yard, not knowing where she was. It wasn't so nice, though, that Mattie had gotten in trouble for tramping on Mom's flowers. He wished now that he had been more careful when he'd guided Mattie around the yard, and he probably shouldn't have let go of her arm.

Mark stared up toward the loft at the rafters overhead and watched as a spider spun its web. *Maybe I'll go see if I can find a bug to put in the spider's web,* he decided. *After all, the poor thing needs to eat, and I don't see any flies here in the barn right now. Of course, that could be because Dad hung so many strips of flypaper around the barn.*

Determined to find at least one suitable insect for the spider, Mark left the barn and walked around the yard for a bit. The wind had begun to blow, but the sun was still out. It didn't take long until he spotted a grasshopper that had jumped out of the weeds and onto the wagon wheel propped against the barn.

Walking slowly toward the wheel, Mark leaned in carefully and made a quick grab for the bug. He knew he'd caught it when he felt the jagged legs of the grasshopper looking for an escape inside his cupped hands.

Once Mark was back in the barn, he climbed up into the hayloft and studied the web. Even though it hung just over from the loft, it was close enough for Mark to throw the bug in and watch what would happen next.

Mark had always liked investigating things, so he intently watched as the insect stuck fast to the spider's web and began to squirm. Mark had the perfect perch there in the loft. In fact, he was almost eye level with the web. It was like having a front-row seat.

In no time at all, the spider apparently felt the vibration of the web and moved in to claim its prey. Mark watched in fascination as the spider quickly spun some of its webbing around the grasshopper, and then went back to its original task of building and repairing other parts of the web.

I suppose that old grasshopper will get eaten sometime later, Mark thought, giving the spider one more glance before climbing back down the ladder. After he'd taken a seat on the bale of straw again, he took his wooden yo-yo out of his pocket and played with that awhile. He was getting pretty good with the different tricks he could do with the yo-yo, especially the one called "walking the dog."

It wasn't long before Mark became tired of playing with the yo-yo. "Sure wish there was something really fun to do," he mumbled. *Wish Mattie would come out here to play. I'll bet she would have freaked out watching that sly old spider trap the grasshopper in its web. But boy, I sure thought it was neat.*

Mark was glad it was still summer, and they wouldn't have to go back to school for a few more weeks, but for the last several days he'd become bored. If he told Mom or Dad that, they'd probably find some job for him to do around the house or yard, so he guessed it would be better if he just sat here—even if he was really bored.

Meow! Meow! Mark's cat, Lucky, rubbed against his leg.

Mark reached down and rubbed a spot behind Lucky's silky ears.

The big, fluffy gray cat started to purr and leaned in closer for more attention.

Any other time Mark would have enjoyed petting Lucky and listening to her purr. Not today, though. Mark wasn't in the mood for sitting and petting. He wanted to do something fun and daring, and it was always better if you had someone to share the excitement with.

Lucky took a few steps, like she was going to walk away, but then she dropped to the floor and rolled over onto her back. Lying there with all four feet in the air, she looked at Mark as if to say, "Aren't you going to rub my big belly?"

Mark gave the cat a couple of pats. "That's all you get for now, Lucky."

Lucky let out a pathetic meow—and plodded away, her belly almost dragging on the cement floor. In another week or so she'd give birth to a batch of kittens, and Mark could hardly wait. He hoped Mom and Dad would let him keep at least one. New kittens were always so cute and a lot of fun.

Glancing around the barn, Mark spotted a big black umbrella leaning against the wall near the door. Dad used it to escort Mom out to the buggy whenever it was raining real hard.

Bet that old umbrella would make a good parachute, Mark thought. He'd never seen a real parachute, except for a picture of one he'd discovered in a magazine at the dentist's office. The umbrella was a lot smaller than a parachute, of course, but with the way the wind was blowing outside, he figured the umbrella would work just as well.

Mark mulled things over in his head a few more minutes; then he jumped up, ran across the room, and snatched the umbrella. After looking it over real good he realized that it was almost like new and didn't have any holes in it. *I bet four people could fit under this big umbrella with no trouble at all. Hmm. . . I wonder if I could talk Mattie into using it as a parachute. Think I'll go ask.*

Mark leaned the umbrella against the bale of straw and hurried out the door, ducking, as two swallows flew swiftly out of the barn. "Hey Mattie," he hollered, startling his twin sister and causing her to jump when he squatted down beside her. "Wanna play a new game with me? It's one we haven't played before, and I promise it'll be exciting and a lot of fun."

"The last game we played sure wasn't fun. Not for me, anyways. " Mattie slowly shook her head. "I sure don't need any more excitement like that."

"I'm sorry about all that. I promise this game will be different, 'cause it's the most exciting game we've ever played."

Mattie, looking a bit more interested now, said, "What's the name of this game?"

"It's called 'flying high.' "

Mattie's forehead wrinkled as her eyebrows pulled together. "I've never heard of a game by that name."

"That's 'cause it's a new game, and we've never played it before."

Mattie shook her head. "No thanks. I don't think I want to play another one of your games."

"But this game is different." Mark gave Mattie's arm a little tug. "Come on, Mattie. You'll see—it'll be lots of fun!"

"Oh, all right, but this game had better not get me in trouble like the last one did."

"I'm sure it won't." Mark pulled Mattie to her feet, took hold of her hand, and they ran into the barn.

"Wait right here while I get the parachute," Mark said. He glanced up at the rafters near the loft. "Oh, and while you're waiting, check out that spider up there and see if it ate the grasshopper I threw into its web awhile ago."

Mattie tipped her head and looked up at the loft. "I'm not sure I want to see any spider eating a bug. That's pretty disgusting."

"No, it's not. It was interesting how that spider spun a web around the grasshopper. It happened so fast, you wouldn't believe it."

Mattie looked at him like he'd lost his mind. "Well I'm not interested in seeing anything like that, but what about this parachute you mentioned? We don't have a parachute, Mark."

"Jah, we do. It's right there." Mark pointed to the umbrella, propped against the bale of straw he'd been sitting on earlier.

"That's not a parachute; it's an umbrella," Mattie said.

"I know, but I'm sure it'll work like a parachute. I checked it over real good, and there are no holes in it either."

Mattie shook her head. "Don't be silly, Mark. We're not going to be jumping out of an airplane, and even if we were, we wouldn't use an umbrella for a parachute."

"I realize that," Mark said. "We'll be jumping off the roof of the chicken coop." He grinned widely. "You can go first, and then I'll give it a try."

Mattie's blue eyes widened, and she blinked a couple of times. "No way! I'm not jumping off any roof, and neither should you. That would be dangerous!"

"We won't get hurt. We'll have the umbrella to slow down our fall. Besides, think how much fun it'll be to float down to the ground. I'll bet it will feel just like we're flying. Better yet, we'll have a soft landing because we'll be jumping into that pile of hay Dad put on the back side of the coop the other day."

Mattie shook her head a little harder this time. "I am not jumping off the roof of the chicken coop! If you think Mom was mad about the flowers, think how upset she'll be if she finds out that we jumped off the roof of the chicken coop. Besides, why would you want to risk hurting yourself? And another thing. . . Why would you want me to go first?"

"Slow down, Mattie. You're getting all worked up for nothing." Mark shrugged and then put his hands on his hips. "But suit yourself if you don't wanna try it. I'm not gonna get hurt, and you're the one who's gonna miss out on knowing what it's like to fly. Besides, no one can see us from up there, so we won't get caught either."

"Mark, you really oughtta think things through before you try such a stunt. I don't wanna know how to fly. Birds fly; people walk, and I'm not a bird." Mattie scowled at him.

"I'm not a bird either, but I am gonna find out what it feels like to be one, and since we're twins, I think you should try it, too. Just imagine what our friends will say when they learn what we can do."

"No way! I don't care what anyone says—I am not crazy enough to jump off the roof and probably end up getting hurt. But if you want to do something so foolish, then go right ahead."

"Will you at least climb up on the roof of the chicken coop with me?" Mark asked.

"I suppose I can do that, but only to watch."

Mark hurried to get the umbrella and then he handed it to Mattie. "Here, hold this while I get the ladder so we can climb on top of the chicken coop."

"This is really *dumm*," Mattie mumbled as she held on to the umbrella and followed Mark out of the barn and over to the chicken coop. "Jah, it's really a dumb idea."

When Mark set the ladder in place and climbed onto the roof, she mumbled even louder, "If Mom and Dad find out about this, you'll be in big trouble—and I'm worried that you'll get hurt."

"They won't find out. Mom went over to Grandpa and Grandma Miller's to pick up Ada and Perry, remember? And Dad and Ike are way out in the field today fixing fences," Mark called over his shoulder. "And quit talking about me getting hurt, 'cause I'm sure I won't."

"What about Calvin or Russell? If they see us, they're sure to tell Mom or Dad about this."

"No they won't. They're selling produce from our roadside stand today, so none of them can even see what we're doing."

"Oh, that's right. Still. . . I don't know about this crazy notion you have."

"Will you relax? I'll be fine, really." He figured once he'd shown Mattie how much fun flying could be, she'd want to give it a try, too.

When Mark stepped onto the roof of the chicken coop, he looked down to be sure the stack of hay was still there. Sure enough, the hay was right where Dad had put it earlier this week.

"Are you sure you don't want to fly like a bird?" he asked Mattie, who now stood beside him, eyes wide and looking really frightened.

She shook her head. "It's gotten awfully windy, and I still don't think you should do this, Mark."

"The wind is exactly what we need." Mark held out his hand. "Just stop talking and give me the umbrella."

Mattie handed it to Mark, and just as he opened it up—*woosh!*—a big gust of wind almost lifted him off his feet.

Mark wobbled, and the wind pushed him back. . . back. . .back, toward the other side of the roof.

"Look at me! I'm fly. . .ing high!" Mark shouted as

another gust of wind lifted him straight up. And then he was falling. . .down. . .down. . .down. . .until—*splat!*—he landed in something soft and squishy, but he knew right away that it wasn't hay.

"Phew! What is that horrible odor?" He slowly exhaled and opened his eyes. "Oh no! I've landed in a pile of stinky manure!"

Chapter 2

A Hard Lesson

Mattie looked down at Mark and gasped when she saw him sitting in the middle of the manure pile. "Oh Mark, are you okay?" she hollered.

"No, I'm not okay! I just landed in manure!"

"Are you hurt?"

"I—I don't think so." As Mark stepped out of the manure pile, lifting one foot, and then the other, it made a squishy sound. "Nothin' seems to be broken. But I'm sure a big mess. And, *phew!*—this malodorous stuff really stinks!"

Mattie plugged her nose. She might not know what *malodorous* meant, but even from up here on the roof of the chicken coop she could smell the stench. "I'll be right there!" she shouted down to Mark.

Mattie scurried down the ladder, and raced around to the other side of the coop. Poor Mark stood there, slowly shaking his head. He really was a mess. Globs of gooey manure clung to his shirt and pants, and some of it was stuck between his bare toes.

"You look *baremlich*," she said, trying not to laugh.

"I know I look terrible, and I feel just as bad. Guess I'd better get in the house and take a shower right away, before Mom gets home and Dad and Ike come in from the fields," Mark said.

"Huh-uh! No way! You'll track manure into the house. Better let me wet you down with the hose first."

Before Mark had a chance to respond, Mattie raced across the yard and turned on the hose. Then she dragged it back through the grass and aimed it right at Mark, blasting his shirt, pants, and bare feet with plenty of water.

"Hey, that's really cold!" Mark jumped up and down.

"Of course it's cold. It's water from the hose, so what did you expect?" Mattie shot another stream of water at her brother while trying to stifle a giggle. "If you don't hold still, I'll never get all that manure washed off!"

Mark continued to hop up and down as she pelted him with more water. "Ye-ow! Think I'm gonna freeze to death!" he hollered.

"Oh, don't be such a *boppli*."

"I'm not a baby, and I bet you're enjoying this, aren't you?"

" 'Course not." *Well, maybe a little,* Mattie thought. "Just hold still!"

Mark rushed toward Mattie, grabbed the hose from her hand, and turned the water on her.

"Absatz! Absatz! That's really, really cold!"

"I'll stop when you promise not to spray me with any more water." Mark looked down at his clothes. "Most of the manure's off anyways, and I'm sick of bein' cold.

Thanks to you, I have goose bumps on top of goose bumps!"

"You'd better get in the house and take a shower now," Mattie said, smiling. "You'll warm up then."

Mark shook his head. "I ain't gonna drip water on Mom's clean floors, so I'd better stay out here in the sun and dry off first, before I go in the house to take a shower."

"Aren't, Mark."

He tipped his head to the right. "Aren't Mark, what?"

She tipped her head to the left. "Huh?"

"I don't know. You said, 'aren't Mark,' and I just asked, 'aren't Mark, what?' "

She shook her finger at him, the way Mom often did when she was scolding one of her seven children. "Stop trying to confuse me. The reason I said 'aren't' is because you said 'ain't,' and *ain't* isn't good English."

Mark grunted. "Now you're confusing me."

"No, I'm the one who's confused, and I think—"

Mattie's words were halted by the *clip-clop* sound of horses' hooves approaching in the distance. She glanced at the road, then back at Mark. "Uh-oh. You're in big trouble now. Mom's home."

The wind had calmed down to just a breeze, and as the horse and buggy got closer, Mattie watched Mom push a strand of auburn hair back under her black outer bonnet that had blown loose.

Mark raced for the house. Mattie was right beside him.

They'd only made it halfway there when Mom, who had just pulled her horse and buggy up to the hitching rail near the barn, hollered, "Absatz!"

Mark screeched to a stop, and when Mattie bumped into his back she plugged her nose. "Phew! You sure do *schtinke*!"

"I wouldn't stink if that gust of wind hadn't pushed me to the wrong side of the chicken coop."

"I know, and when it lifted you into the air, I was really scared."

"Not me. I wasn't scared till I landed in that pile of manure."

"Phew! What's that awful smell?" Mom asked as she approached the twins. Three-year-old Ada and five-year-old Perry held on to her hands. Mom looked at Mark's clothes, where a few blobs of manure still clung, and frowned. "What have you been doing? Have you two been up to mischief again?"

"Not me," said Mattie. "Mark sort of—well, he landed in the manure pile when he was seeing if he could. . ."

Mom's eyebrows shot up as she stared at Mark. "What on earth is your sister talking about? Why would you be playing in a pile of smelly manure?"

"I wasn't playing in it, Mom. I was trying to show Mattie how to use Dad's big umbrella as a parachute, so we climbed onto the roof of the chicken coop, and—"

"The wind came up and pushed Mark backward," Mattie said, finishing Mark's sentence. "Then another gust of wind lifted him into the air, and when he came down, he landed in the pile of manure."

Perry started to laugh, but Mom's mouth dropped open, and her blue eyes widened in disbelief. "You—you did what?"

"Well, I thought I could fly, and since there was hay on the ground where I was gonna jump, I didn't think I'd get hurt." Mark paused and gulped in some air. "I—I sure didn't think the wind would push me over to the other side of the roof, or that I'd end up landing where the pile of manure was."

Mom's frown deepened, and she let go of Perry and Ada's hands so she could shake her finger at Mark. "You ought to know better than to do something so foolish and dangerous. Why, you could have been seriously hurt!"

Mark hung his head, feeling really foolish. Mom was right, he could have gotten hurt. "Sorry, Mom," he mumbled. "I know it was dumm and I'll never do it again."

"I should say not," Mom said with a click of her tongue. She pointed to the house. "Now get inside and take a shower. Oh, and put your smelly clothes in a plastic bag. I don't want them stinking up the other clothes in the laundry basket."

"What about the umbrella?" Mark asked. "It's still in the manure pile, and I—I think it's broken."

"Just leave it there for now. I'll have your *daed* take care of it," Mom said. "But of course, if it is broken, you'll need to buy a new one."

"But Mom, I don't have enough money to buy another umbrella," Mark argued.

"Then I'm sure your daed will find some extra chores

for you to do so you can earn the money," Mom added as she took Ada and Perry's hands again and moved toward the house. "In fact, if he doesn't find some chores for you, then I certainly will!" she called over her shoulder.

Mark shot Mattie a quick glance, wondering if she was glad he'd been the one to get yelled at this time, and then he hurried into the house behind Mom. He was lucky she hadn't given him a worse punishment. And he definitely wanted to get cleaned up before Dad came in from the fields and saw what he'd gotten into.

During supper that evening, Mattie looked over at Mark and noticed a strange expression on his face. He hadn't said a word since they'd started eating their meal. Was he dreading the extra chores Dad had given him to do because of all the mischief, or was there something else on her twin brother's mind? Maybe she would let Mark off the hook and not make him wash the dishes for her tonight.

"Won't be long now and you'll be going back to school," Dad said, touching Mattie's arm. "Are you ready to begin the third grade?"

"Wish I didn't have to go back to school," Mattie said. "I can't wait till I graduate from eighth grade and get to stay home with Mom all day."

"Staying home with your *mamm* won't be as easy as you think," Dad said, handing Mattie the basket of homemade bread.

"That's right," Mom said with a nod. "Learning how to be a good homemaker will mean a lot more chores, as well as learning to do many things you haven't done before."

"Like what?" Mattie wanted to know.

"Like sewing, quilting, baking, and cooking meals." Dad handed Mattie the bowl of mashed potatoes. "You'll need to know how to do those things before you get married."

Mattie scrunched up her nose. "Don't see why I'd have to learn all that, 'cause I'm never gettin' married. Boys are weird, and they do dumm things."

Dad chuckled and gave Mattie's shoulder a pat. "You'll change your mind about that someday."

Mattie didn't think so, but she decided not to say anything more about it, because graduating from school was still a ways off, and it would be several years before she was even old enough to think about marriage.

Mattie glanced across the table at her oldest brother, Ike. She had learned that when Ike was her age, his hair used to be bright red like hers and Mark's. But since then his hair had grown darker and turned a deep auburn color like Mom's. Ike had recently started going out with a girl named Catherine. Mattie had never heard him say anything about wanting to get married though. Of course, Ike was only sixteen, so he probably wouldn't think about getting married for a few more years. Then there was Russell, who'd turned thirteen in April, and Calvin, who was eleven. It was obvious who they took after. Their hair was as blond as Dad's. And as far as Mattie knew they had no interest in girls, other than to tease them, the way Mark often did.

Mattie looked over at Mark. He still hadn't said anything, and she couldn't figure it out. It wasn't like him to be so quiet.

She gave his arm a little nudge with her elbow. "How come you're not saying anything?"

"Can't think of anything to say," he mumbled around a piece of Mom's juicy fried chicken. "Besides, can't you see that I'm eatin' my supper?"

"We're all eating, but we're all talkin', too," Mattie said.

Mark grabbed the meat platter and forked another piece of chicken onto his plate.

Mattie continued to eat her meal as she listened to Mom and Dad talk about some things that had been going on in their community lately. When she got bored with their conversation she turned her attention to her little brother, Perry, whose hair was so blond it was the color of the palomino horse down the road from where they lived. She watched as Perry fed Ada his green beans. Mattie knew Perry didn't like green beans, but apparently Ada did, for she was chomping away and smacking her lips as if the beans tasted like candy.

Mattie giggled to herself, seeing the green beans stuck in Ada's red hair. It looked almost as funny as the time Ada had dumped a bowl of macaroni on her head.

Mom and Dad didn't seem to notice what was going on, because they were talking about Dad's woodworking business, and how many orders he'd recently gotten for new tables and chairs. Mattie thought about interrupting their conversation to tell them what Perry was doing, but figured she'd probably be accused of being a tattletale if she did, so she decided it would be best to keep quiet.

As Mattie ate, she wondered if there was a way she could get out of going to school. She liked their teacher, Anna Ruth Stutzman, well enough, and she enjoyed playing with her best friend, Stella Schrock, during recess. What she didn't like about school was learning her multiplication tables and trying to spell difficult words. Mark didn't have a problem with either of those. In fact he could spell words that Mattie couldn't even pronounce. It was funny how one minute Mark would use some big word, and the next minute he'd say "ain't," which even Mattie knew wasn't proper English.

He probably just does that to irritate me, Mattie thought.

Mark reached over just then and tickled Ada under her chin. Ada giggled and started waving her hands, like she always did when she got overly excited.

"Not now," Mom scolded, looking over at Mark. "This isn't the time or place to be fooling around. If Ada gets too excited she might knock something over. And how'd those beans get in her hair?"

Shrugging his shoulders, Mark stopped tickling Ada and reached for another piece of chicken. Mattie couldn't believe he could eat so much food.

"Would someone please pass me the sugar bowl?" Mom asked. "I didn't put enough sweetener in my iced tea."

"Jah, sure." Mattie reached for the sugar bowl and quickly passed it to Mom.

As soon as Mom lifted the lid on the bowl there was a—*Ribbit! Ribbit!*—then a little frog, covered in sugar, hopped out of the bowl and landed on the table with a thud!

Mom screamed so loud that Ada flinched and started crying. Even the green beans fell out of her hair. Then Dad leaned forward and grabbed hold of the frog. "Alright now," he said with a very stern look, "who's the one responsible for putting that *frosch* in the sugar bowl?"

No one said a word. Mattie and her brothers just sat there. She knew for certain that it hadn't been Ada, because she was too little to do something like that. Same for Perry. And Ike was old enough to know better, so that left Russell, Calvin, or Mark.

"Well, who did it?" Dad asked again, squinting his brown eyes as he looked at each of the children.

Mark's cheeks reddened as he hung his head. "I'm the one who put the frosch in the sugar bowl," he admitted. "It was supposed to be a joke, and I never thought Mom would. . ."

"You about startled me out of my wits," Mom said. "What in the world were you thinking?"

Before Mark could respond, Dad pushed his chair away from the table. Then, looking down at Mark with a deep frown, he said, "I'm going to put the frosch outside. You'd better finish your supper quick, because when I get back, we're going to settle this matter."

CHAPTER 3

Spilled Milk and Sour Juice

"Dad was pretty upset with you last night, wasn't he?" Mattie asked when she met Mark in the hallway outside their bedrooms the following morning.

Mark nodded. "Jah, and because of the umbrella stunt and me putting the frosch in the sugar bowl, I've gotta clean out the chicken coop every day for a week and do some other extra chores, too."

"I hope you learned a good lesson," she said, squinting at him, the way Mom did when she was scolding someone.

Mark frowned. "I don't need a lecture from you, Mattie. I know puttin' that frosch in the sugar bowl was wrong, and thinkin' I could fly was really dumm. I sure won't do either of those things again. Just wanted to have a little fun, that's all."

"Your idea of fun is sure strange, but it's good you're not going to do anything like that again, 'cause I think it really scared Mom."

"Didn't mean to scare her. It was meant for you." Mark snickered. "Just thought it'd be funny to see your expression when you opened the lid and saw that little amphibian."

"Oh, so that 'amphibian,' which I guess means 'frog,' was meant for me, huh?"

Mark gave a nod.

She poked his arm. "You tease too much, Mark. And for your information, *Ich verschreck net graad.*"

Mark scrunched up his nose. "Well, you may not frighten easily, but I'm sure you would have been startled if that little ol' frog had jumped in your plate."

Mattie nodded. "I wouldn't have liked that at all."

"I'm sorry," Mark said as he hurried out the door to do his chores.

When Mattie entered the kitchen, she found Mom in front of their propane-operated stove, frying hickory-smoked bacon.

"Umm. . .that sure smells good," Mattie said, smacking her lips. "Are we having fried *oier* to go with it?"

Mom shook her head. "I'm low on eggs this morning, so I've decided to make *pannekuche* to go with the bacon."

"Pancakes are my favorite thing to have for breakfast." Mattie's mouth watered just thinking about all that melted butter and warm maple syrup drizzled over a stack of big fluffy pancakes. "How come we're low on eggs? Are the chickens sick?"

"It could be they sense the cooler weather coming, or it could be because our chickens are getting older," Mom explained. "As chickens age, they lay fewer eggs."

"Maybe we can get some little peeps to raise so

we can have more egg-layers," Mattie suggested. She thought it would be fun to have some baby chicks.

"Well, we probably won't think about that until springtime. Winter will be coming sooner than we think, and the cold weather can be too harsh on baby animals," Mom said. "Now, why don't you get started setting the table while I mix the pancake batter? We'll eat as soon as your daed and the boys come in from doing their chores."

Mattie knew that Dad and her brother Ike would head for the woodshop as soon as they'd eaten. Now that the hay was all cut, they wouldn't be spreading manure in the fields until autumn, which was still a few weeks away. So until then, most of their time would be spent in the shop.

Mattie wasn't sure what Mark, Russell, and Calvin had planned for the day. She'd made her own plans, however. Right after breakfast, once the dishes were done, she planned to pick some daisies and decorate the porch railing, as well as the fence that separated their driveway from the alfalfa pasture.

"Where's Ada and Perry?" Mattie asked as she began setting the table. "I figured they'd be in here waiting to eat. Seems like those two are always *hungerich*."

"You're right about them always being hungry." Mom chuckled. "Perry went out to the barn to see if Lucky's had her *busslin* yet, and Ada's still sleeping."

Mattie wrinkled her nose. "I hope you can find a home for all the kittens, 'cause we don't need any more *katze* around here."

"Since it's Mark's cat he'll probably want to keep one of the kittens, but we'll try to find homes for the rest of Lucky's babies."

Mattie wished her dog, Twinkles, would have some puppies. As far as she was concerned, a puppy was a lot more fun to play with than a kitten. A pup could be trained to do tricks, too. Mattie had been working with Twinkles, and she could already do several good tricks, like roll over, sit, and play dead. The only thing Mark's cat did was eat, sleep, purr, and scratch. Of course, she did catch some mice now and then.

Mattie winced, thinking about the last time she'd been scratched by Lucky. She'd heard the way the cat purred whenever Mark stroked her belly, but when Mattie tried doing that a few weeks ago, Lucky hissed, stuck out her claws, and scratched Mattie's hand. That was the last time Mattie went anywhere near Mark's annoying cat!

By the time Mattie finished setting the table, Mom had the pancake batter mixed. "If you'll go wake Ada, I'll start making the pancakes."

"Okay, Mom." Mattie left the kitchen and tromped up the stairs to Ada's room. She found her little sister curled up at the foot of the bed, with her sheet wrapped around her feet. Her flushed cheeks almost matched her flaming red hair.

"Wake up, sleepyhead." Mattie gently poked Ada's arm.

Ada opened her eyes, but they were just tiny slits. "*Is fattgange*, Mattie."

"I'm not going away." Mattie bent down and tickled Ada's feet. "Mom has breakfast almost ready. It's time to get up."

Ada closed her eyes and pulled the sheet over her head.

Mattie pulled the sheet aside and shook her sister's arm. "Mom's making pannekuche."

Ada's eyes opened wide and she leaped out of bed. "Yum! Yum!"

"You doin' alright today?" Russell asked Mark as they left the barn and followed Dad, Ike, Calvin, and Perry toward the house.

"Jah, sure. Why do you ask?"

"Figured you might be feelin' out of sorts," Russell said, keeping his voice so low, only Mark could hear. "After getting in trouble with Dad last night I can sure understand, 'cause I've been in your shoes a few times myself."

"I'm fine." Mark didn't want to talk about this again. He just wanted to forget he'd ever put that frog in the sugar bowl and been punished for it. It probably seemed to Mom and Dad that he'd been misbehaving a little too much lately. But really, all Mark wanted to do was have some fun.

Russell thumped Mark's back. "Say, how'd ya like to go fishin' with me and Calvin later this morning? We're going to the pond by our neighbor's place."

Mark grinned at his brother. "Sure, that'd be great."

"All right then, after Dad and Ike leave for work, we'll get our fishing poles and head for the pond."

Mark felt pretty good about going fishing, and when he entered the house and smelled hickory-smoked bacon and maple syrup, he felt even better.

"Did Lucky have her busslin yet?" Mom asked.

Mark shook his head. "She was in her box though, so I bet it'll be soon."

Mom smiled. "Well, wash up now and take a seat," she said, motioning to the table. "The pancakes are done, and we're ready to eat."

After everyone was seated at the table, they bowed their heads for silent prayer. Mark asked God to bless the food and help him catch lots of fish today.

When the prayers were finished, Mom passed the platters of pancakes and bacon around.

Mark reached for the maple syrup and was getting ready to pour it on his pancakes when he bumped Mattie's elbow as she was about to pick up her glass of milk. *Thunk!* The glass toppled over and milk spilled onto the table.

"Oh no!" Mark and Mattie both groaned.

"It's okay. I'll take care of it," Mom said, rising from her seat.

While Mom wiped up the mess with a dishtowel, Mattie turned to Mark and said, "Can't you be more careful?"

"Sorry," Mark said. "Guess if you were right-handed like me, we wouldn't be bumping arms."

Mattie grinned. "Or if you were left-handed like me,

47

we wouldn't be bumping arms."

"Mark can trade places with Calvin," Mom said.

"That won't work," Calvin spoke up, " 'Cause I'm right-handed, too."

"You're left-handed," Dad said to Russell. "Why don't you trade places with Mark?"

"Okay." Russell left his chair and exchanged seats with Mark.

Mom handed Dad the platter of bacon. "While I'm up getting Mattie another glass of *melke*, would anyone else like some?"

"I'd rather have orange juice," Mark said.

"Are you sure about that?" Mom asked. "The orange juice will taste sour after eating pancakes and sweet maple syrup."

"I'm sure it'll be good." Mark smacked his lips. "I really do like orange juice."

"Very well, then." Mom went to the refrigerator and took out two pitchers—one with milk in it, and one full of orange juice. She poured Mark a glass of orange juice and handed it to him, just as he finished eating his pancake.

Mark took a big drink and puckered his lips. "Yuck! This juice is really sour!" He set his glass down. "I've changed my mind. Can I have some melke now?"

"Jah, you can, but not until you've finished your orange juice," Dad said. "We don't waste food or drink around here, and your mamm did warn you about the orange juice being sour."

Mark drank his juice down as fast as he could.

He'd just finished the last of it, and was reaching for the pitcher of milk, when Ada knocked over her glass. *Splat!*—icy cold milk went all over Mark's plate and ran onto his clothes.

"This is not starting off to be a very good day," Mark mumbled as he raced up the stairs to change his clothes. "Sure hope the rest of my day goes better!"

CHAPTER 4

Missing!

As soon as Mattie finished helping Mom with the dishes, she hurried outside to pick some of the pretty white daisies growing under the fence along the edge of the alfalfa pasture. As she picked the flowers, she sang a little song she'd made up.

"Daisy. . .daisy. . .pretty little daisy. . .your center is yellow. . .your petals are white. God made you, daisy, to look just right."

"Ah-hem! What do you think you're doin' with those posies?"

Mattie dropped a flower and whirled around. Mark stood behind her staring into the basket of daisies she'd already picked, with one eyebrow raised and a smirk on his face.

"Don't sneak up on me like that, and they're not posies—they're daisies."

"Well, whatever they're called, how come you're pickin' so many of them?" he questioned.

"I'm going to decorate the fence."

"With the flowers?"

"Of course with the flowers."

"I think that's girl stuff, Mattie," Mark said.

"Maybe so, but I want everything to look pretty when Grandma and Grandpa Miller come for supper this evening. They'll see the flowers when they come up the driveway with their horse and buggy."

Mark shrugged his shoulders. "Well, if you want to put posies on the fence, that's up to you, but I'm goin' fishin' with Calvin and Russell. Do you wanna come with us?"

"No thanks," Mattie said as she wrapped the stem of a daisy around the fence post.

After the boys left, Mattie continued to sing her little song as she added more colorful daisies to the fence. She'd just finished the last one, and was about to start putting flowers on the porch railing, when her best friend, Stella Schrock, rode in on her bicycle.

"Whatcha doin'?" Stella asked after she'd parked her bike near the porch.

"I decorated the fence with daisies, and now I'm going to put some on the porch railing," Mattie said with a smile.

"Can I help you with that?" Stella asked.

Mattie nodded.

"How come you're decorating the fence and the porch railing with flowers?"

Mattie explained that her grandparents were coming for supper and she wanted everything to look nice.

Stella smiled. "That makes sense to me."

Sometimes, like now, Mattie thought she and Stella

were more like twins than she and Mark. They liked many of the same things, and Stella wasn't a big tease who liked to play tricks. She didn't use big words like Mark did either. Of course, Stella didn't look anything like Mattie. She had dark brown hair and matching eyes, and there was not one freckle on her nose.

As the girls wrapped the flower stems around the porch railing, they talked about school, how it would be starting up again in a few weeks, and how much they'd miss staying at home.

"The reason I don't like school is because I have a hard time learning some things, and Mark always does so well—especially with spelling," Mattie said. "He knows so many big words, and hardly ever misses any of the words on our spelling tests. Sometimes I feel really dumm when I'm around my twin bruder— especially when he uses big words I can't even say. I think he just does it for attention," she said. "It probably makes him feel big and important if he can say words I don't understand."

"Do you think Mark is full of *hochmut*?" Stella asked.

Mattie shrugged. "He might be full of pride, but we're taught in our church that it's wrong to be prideful, so if he is, then he's not setting a good example to others."

"That's true, but nobody's perfect," Stella said.

Mattie gave a nod.

"Are you excited about your ninth birthday coming up soon?" Stella asked, changing the subject.

"I sure am, and I'm hoping for a bicycle. Mark wants

one, too. Even though we live fairly close to the school, it would be a lot quicker for us to get there every day if we didn't have to walk."

"I know. I'm thankful for the bike my folks gave me for Christmas last year," Stella said. "I can pedal to school in half the time it took me to walk. And I don't have to carry my schoolbooks now, because there's a basket on my bike."

"Mark and I have both mentioned to Mom and Dad that we'd like a bicycle, so I hope they've been listening. If I get a bike with a basket, I'll decorate it with flowers. 'Course Mark will probably say that's girl stuff," Mattie said. "But then he does a lot of boy stuff I'd never do, too."

Mattie proceeded to tell Stella how Mark had been lifted off the roof of the chicken coop using Dad's umbrella and landed in a pile of manure.

Stella wrinkled her nose. "Eww. . .that must have smelled baremlich. I bet he looked pretty funny sitting in that awful stuff."

"You're right, he did smell terrible, and he looked really funny. It was hard for me not to laugh, 'cause it really served him right." Mattie snickered. "Mom wasn't happy about the smelly clothes or the broken umbrella, but at least Mark didn't get hurt."

Then Mattie told Stella how Mark had put the frog in the sugar bowl, hoping to scare her with it. "Dad wasn't happy about him startling Mom like that, and now Mark has extra chores to do," she added.

"I think he had it coming after doing two bad things in one day." Stella shook her head slowly. "Sometimes my bruder does things that get him in trouble."

"Guess we girls do, too, but since Mark's such a big tease and likes to play tricks, he gets in trouble a lot more than I do." Mattie stopped talking and took in a quick breath; then she went on to tell Stella about the little game she and Mark had played with her being blindfolded and how she'd ended up ruining some of Mom's flowers.

"It sounds like that game wasn't much fun at all."

"Nope, it sure wasn't."

"Looks like we're out of flowers," Stella said, changing the subject. "So can we do something else now?"

"What do you want to do?" Mattie asked.

"Why don't we go up to your room and play with your dolls?"

"Sure, let's go."

The girls raced into the house and hurried up the stairs to Mattie's bedroom.

"You sure keep your room nice," Stella said. "Everything looks so neat and tidy."

Mattie smiled. "I'm not like Mark. I don't like having a messy room. Mom has to remind him all the time to pick up his room and put his things away where they belong, but he doesn't seem to care about things like that."

"I don't like a cluttered room either," Stella agreed. "I clean mine at least once a week."

Mattie got out two of her favorite dolls, and as the girls took seats on Mattie's bed, the sun shone brightly through her bedroom windows, making it extra light in the room. Both dolls had cloth bodies, but their heads, arms, and legs were made of vinyl. They were dressed in Amish clothes and looked almost like real babies.

"I can't wait till I grow up and have a boppli of my own," Stella said. "Babies are soft and cuddly, and they smell so sweet."

Mattie wrinkled her nose. "Not when they mess their *windle*."

"That's true," Stella agreed. "No one likes to change dirty diapers."

They'd only been playing a little while when Mom stuck her head in the open doorway. "Perry and I will be heading to Millersburg now to get him some new shoes," she said. "So I'm going to send Ada up here to play with you and Stella."

Mattie's eyebrows shot up. "What? Aren't you taking Ada with you?"

Mom shook her head. "She gets restless when we go shopping, and it would be hard for me to keep her occupied and help Perry try on shoes. Besides, I told you earlier that I'd need your help and would be leaving Ada with you for a while. Did you forget?"

"Jah." Mattie wasn't the least bit happy about watching her little sister, but with Stella there to help, maybe it wouldn't be so bad.

"Come on, Stella. Let's go downstairs," Mattie said, after Mom left the room.

"How come?" Stella asked with a curious expression. "I thought we were gonna play with your dolls."

"Didn't you hear what my mamm said? I have to watch Ada while she's gone."

"Can't you watch her up here?"

Mattie shook her head so hard that the ribbon ties on her head covering swished around her face. "Ada's even messier than Mark, and I don't want her in my room. Besides, if she comes in here she'll want to play with my dolls, and I won't allow that at all."

"Why not?"

" 'Cause she doesn't know how to be careful with things, and I don't want my dolls to get ruined." Mattie set her doll on the bench near the window. "Let's go downstairs. We can find something else to do while Mom and Perry are gone."

When they got downstairs, they found Mom standing by the back door with Perry. "Our driver's here now, so we're heading out."

"Okay, but where's Ada?" Mattie questioned.

"She was hungry, so I fixed her some cheese and crackers." Mom motioned to the kitchen. "When she's done eating, make sure her hands get washed. Oh, and Mattie. . .there's one more thing. Be sure you keep a close watch on Ada. You know how she likes to wander off."

Mattie nodded. "Since Stella's here we can both watch Ada."

Mom gave Mattie a hug and then she and Perry hurried out the door.

"Should we go to the kitchen for a little snack?" Mattie asked Stella.

"That sounds good," Stella said with a nod. "I'm kind of hungerich, too."

When the girls entered the kitchen, they found Ada

sitting on a stool at the table. Since she was too short to sit in a regular chair, the stool was just right for her.

"*Kaes*," Ada said, smiling at Mattie and pointing to the cheese Mom had cut up for her.

"Jah. Stella and I are gonna have some kaes, too." Mattie went to the refrigerator and took out some slices of cheddar cheese. Then she got a box of crackers down from the cupboard.

"Would you like something to drink?" Mattie asked Stella. "How about some melke?"

"Sounds good to me." Stella took a seat at the table and Mattie got out the milk and two glasses.

Mattie had just started to eat when Ada hollered, "Kaes! *Meh* kaes!"

Mattie didn't want to get up for more cheese, so she handed Ada a few pieces from her own plate.

As they ate, they visited some more, and giggled at Ada while listening to her try to sing in German Dutch the words to, "Oh where, oh where, has my little dog gone." It was cute hearing Ada's own version of the song she'd heard their family sing together on many occasions.

"When we're done eating would you like to see some of the tricks I've taught my dog?" Mattie asked Stella.

Stella nodded eagerly. "That sounds like fun. Maybe we can teach Twinkles a few new tricks, too."

After Mattie and Stella were done eating, they took Ada outside, and then Mattie called Twinkles, her little brown-and-white fox terrier, who liked to sleep in the barn.

It took a few minutes of clapping and calling to get

Twinkles's attention. When the dog finally ran out of the barn, Ada started jumping up and down, while waving her hands.

"*Hundli!*" Ada shouted. "Hundli! Hundli!"

"Twinkles is not a puppy, she's two years old." Mattie tapped Ada's shoulder. "And you need to settle down."

Mattie was sure Ada didn't understand what she'd said, because she kept jumping up and down, waving her hands, and hollering at the top of her lungs, "Hundli! Hundli! Hundli!"

"Calm down now, Ada!" Mattie scolded, as she shook her finger. "Twinkles won't do any tricks if you carry on like that."

"What tricks can the dog do?" Stella asked.

"Let me show you." Mattie pointed at Twinkles and said, "Sit!"

Twinkles sat on her haunches and looked up at Mattie with her brown, almond-shaped eyes, as if begging for a treat. *Woof! Woof!*

"Good job, Twinkles," Stella said. She really did look impressed.

Ada squealed and waved her hands some more.

"Roll over," Mattie said, ignoring Ada, and turning her hand in the direction she wanted Twinkles to roll.

Woof! Twinkles's little black nose twitched as she dropped to the ground and rolled one way and then the other.

Stella and Mattie both laughed, but when Twinkles rolled over again, Ada got so excited she started running around in circles, as she continued to wave her hands and holler, "Hundli!"

Woof! Woof! Woof! Twinkles ran behind Ada, barking and leaping into the air like she had springs in her legs.

"Stop it, Twinkles!" Mattie shouted. "Settle down now and come here to me."

Twinkles, paying no attention to Mattie now, continued to run and jump, until she nearly wore herself out and started panting. The poor dog's tongue stuck out on one side of her mouth, but she still kept running and jumping.

"Fox terriers are very energetic dogs and they love to jump," Mattie told Stella. "There are two types— smooth fox terriers and wire fox terriers. You can see by Twinkles's fur that she's a smooth fox terrier. Terriers like her also like to bark, dig, and chase small animals."

"Twinkles is *voll schpass!*" Ada hollered as she danced around the yard waving her hands above her head.

"Jah, I know Twinkles is very funny," Mattie shouted so she could be heard, "but you're getting her all worked up." She raced after the dog, clapping her hands. "Go on back to the barn, Twinkles—right now!"

Woof! Woof! Woof! Twinkles tipped her head to one side, as though thinking about it; then she gave another loud bark and headed straight for the barn.

Mattie was relieved that the dog had obeyed her, however Stella looked disappointed, and Ada started crying. *So much for showing Stella some of Twinkles's tricks!*

"Let's do something else," Mattie said. "Something a little quieter."

"We could go back to your room and play with your dolls," Stella suggested.

Mattie shook her head and motioned to Ada, who was now howling like one of Grandpa Miller's calves when it couldn't find its mother. "No, remember, I said it's better if we don't do that."

Stella shrugged. "If you don't want to play with the dolls, and we can't watch Twinkles do any more tricks, then what can we do?"

"Hmmm. . ." Mattie squinted her eyes and rubbed her chin as she tried to think of something fun to do.

"I know. . . Let's sit on the porch swing and read a *buch*," Stella suggested.

Mattie shook her head. "That'd be boring. Besides, we'll be reading plenty of books when we go back to school. Why don't we lie in the grass and look at the clouds?"

"Huh-uh. I'd rather not."

Mattie snapped her fingers. "I know! We can make some homemade bubble solution and see if we can get Mark's cat, Lucky, to chase them."

"That's a good idea. I'm sure Ada would like blowing bubbles, too." Stella glanced around the yard, and then she looked at Mattie with a worried frown. "Where is Ada?"

"She's right here." Mattie looked down, but Ada was gone. "That makes no sense. She was here a minute ago."

"Maybe she went to the barn to find Twinkles," Stella said.

"You're probably right." Mattie raced into the barn.

"Ada, where are you?" she called, looking all around.

No response; not even a bark or a whine from Twinkles.

Mattie searched in every part of the barn, but there was no sign of Ada. However, she finally found Twinkles curled up in a ball on top of a bale of hay. She figured Ada had to be playing somewhere in the yard, or maybe she was hiding from them.

Mattie was almost to the barn door when she collided with Stella.

"Oops!" Stella rubbed her forehead. "Are you okay, Mattie?"

"Jah, I'm fine. It's just a little bump on the head. How are you?"

"I'll be okay, too. Did you find Ada?"

"No. I think she must be somewhere in the yard. Why don't you go this way, and I'll go that way." Mattie pointed to one side of the yard and then the other. "One of us is bound to find her."

The girls took off in opposite directions. Mattie shielded her eyes from the glare of the sun. No sign of Ada in the alfalfa pasture. "Ada, where are you?" she called.

Mattie kept searching and calling for her little sister. If she didn't find her before Mom got home, she didn't know what she would do. It would be awful to tell Mom that Ada was missing, and Mattie was sure she'd be in trouble for not keeping a closer eye on her little sister.

Another thought popped into Mattie's head. *If Ada wandered off our property and got onto the road, she could get hit by a car!*

Mattie's heart thumped and her palms grew sweaty. Off in the distance she could see dark clouds forming, which meant rain, so she had to find Ada, and quickly!

Chapter 5

A Terrible Day

"How's it going over there?" Mark's brother Calvin called to him from the other side of the pond. "Have you caught any fish?"

Mark cupped his hands around his mouth and hollered, "Nope, not even one. How about you?"

"Not yet, but I've had a few nibbles!"

Mark pointed at Russell, who sat several feet away. "He has two nice-sized fish in his bucket already."

"That's great! At least one of is having some luck," Calvin said.

"Sure wish I'd catch something," Mark mumbled.

"You have to be patient," Russell said. "Or maybe you should move to a different spot."

Mark frowned. He'd already moved to several spots, and none of them seemed any better. At this rate, it didn't look like he'd catch any fish today!

Bzzz. . . Bzzz. . . Mark slapped at a mosquito that had landed on his arm. It seemed like he'd been slapping at them ever since they'd gotten to the pond. If things didn't improve soon, the only thing he'd be taking home would be a whole lot of itchy mosquito bites!

Feeling kind of drowsy, Mark set his fishing pole aside, removed his straw hat, and lay back in the grass. Then, placing his hat over his face, he closed his eyes and thought about the new bicycle he hoped he'd get for his birthday next month. A blue-and-white one would be really nice. He'd also like a carrier on the back of the bike, where he could tie on his schoolbooks. How nice it would be to ride to school every day, like his two older brothers did. Mark knew that Mattie was hoping for a bicycle, too, only she wanted hers to be red.

Mark and Mattie had both been disappointed when they'd learned that Grandpa and Grandma Troyer might not make it for their birthday celebration, which was coming up soon. Grandma and Grandpa lived farther north in a town called Burton, and it was more than one hundred miles away. Since it was too far to travel by horse and buggy, it meant having to hire a driver to bring them to Walnut Creek. That would normally be okay, but in Grandma's last letter she said Grandpa's arthritis had been acting up, and that if he wasn't better by Mark and Mattie's birthday they wouldn't be coming to help them celebrate.

A breeze blew softly over Mark, and he let his mind drift to a time last year when Mom and Dad had surprised them all with a little family getaway. They'd hired a driver with a van and gone to Burton to visit Grandpa and Grandma Troyer and go to the Geauga County Fair. Since the fair was close to Grandpa and Grandma's house, they were able to walk to it. During the day, while Ada and Perry took their naps, Mom and Dad had some quiet time to visit with Grandma and Grandpa while Mark and Mattie went with Calvin, Russell, and Ike to the fairgrounds to take in some of the events. Mark didn't know what he liked best—the rooster crowing contest, the lively music, or all the good food. Of course, he'd saved room for the delicious supper Grandma had cooked. Afterward, Grandpa built a fire outdoors, and they'd all roasted marshmallows.

Thinking about all the fun he'd had made Mark feel even drowsier, and soon he drifted off to sleep, dreaming about toasty marshmallows and a brand-new bike.

"You won't catch any fish like that. You've gotta put your line in the water."

Pushing the hat off his face, Mark's eyes snapped open and he squinted up at Russell, who stood over him with his fishing pole.

"I'm gettin' tired of holding my pole and not catching any fish." Mark's stomach rumbled as he sat up. "I'm hungerich. Wish I'd brought something to snack on." Thinking about all the good food he'd eaten at Grandma and Grandpa Troyer's last year hadn't helped either.

"I think Calvin brought some beef jerky along. Want some of that?" Russell asked.

Mark wrinkled his nose. "Huh-uh. Beef jerky's too tough."

"I have some chewing gum. Would you like a piece?"

Mark shook his head. "Whenever I chew gum it

makes me feel even hungrier. Anyways, I still have a few sticks of gum in my pocket from the pack Grandpa Miller gave me the last time we visited there."

"Well, it's all we've got, so if you already have gum, and don't want any beef jerky, then you'll just have to suffer."

"Maybe I'll go look for some blackberries," Mark said. "I'll bet there are some ripe ones around here by now."

"Probably so, but you came to fish, not pick berries," his brother reminded him.

"But I'm not gettin' any fish, so I may as well pick some berries." Mark plunked his hat back on his head and jumped up. Then he grabbed the plastic bucket he'd brought along, which he'd hoped to fill with fish. Since he hadn't caught any, he figured he may as well put the bucket to good use.

"I'll be back as soon as I have some berries for us to eat," he told Russell. "If there are enough ripe ones, I might get some for Mom, so she can bake a blackberry pie."

Russell smacked his lips and smoothed his shiny blond hair back under his straw hat. "That sounds really good. Just don't be gone too long, 'cause we need to be home in time for supper."

Feeling a little better about things, Mark hurried away. He had a hunch he might be more successful at berry picking than he was at fishing today.

When Mark reached the berry patch, he was pleased to discover lots of plump, ripe berries. The only problem was all the good ones were deep inside the berry patch. The ones near the edge had already been picked by someone else. Or maybe some critter had eaten them. Well, he'd do the best he could and get the ones he could reach.

Mark started picking lickety-split, eating a few of the juicy berries and putting the rest into the bucket. By the time he'd picked all he could reach, the bucket wasn't even half full of berries. He'd need a lot more if he was going to take some home for Mom to bake a pie.

Guess I'll just have to go deeper into the bushes, Mark decided.

He pushed a thorny branch aside and hollered, "Ouch!" when it scratched his arm.

"Ouch! Ouch!" Even through his pant legs he could feel the harsh thorns of the blackberry bush. They seemed to be grabbing at him with every step he took.

I'm tough. I can do this, he told himself. *Can't let a few stickers keep me from getting all those juicy, ripe berries.*

Deeper and deeper into the blackberry bush he went, until a whole bunch of plump, purple berries were within his grasp.

Plunk! Plunk! Plunk! The berries went into the bucket, until it was almost full. Then Mark ate a few more berries, until his stomach was full as well.

"Kumme, Mark! It's time to go!" Calvin called. "Hurry up now, the wind's picking up and it might start to rain!"

"Coming!" Mark hollered, looking up at the sky. He

was surprised to see how cloudy it had gotten when just a short time ago it was nice and sunny.

He took a step forward and realized that he was surrounded by thorny bushes. No matter which way he went he was bound to get all stuck up.

"Oh boy, guess I'm not as tough as I thought I was. Sure wish now I'd never come in here," he muttered. "I need to get out really fast!"

Bzzz. . . Bzzz. . . A big bumblebee buzzed Mark's ear.

He swatted at it, but that only made things worse. The bee left its stinger in Mark's right hand.

"Yeow!" Mark dropped the bucket, and plowing through the bushes, he heard little ripping sounds as the thorns held fast to his shirt and pants.

Finally free of those prickly stickers, he ran screaming all the way back to the pond.

Just as he reached his brothers, a gust of wind came up, and—*swoosh!*—it lifted Mark's hat right off his head. The wind carried his hat this way and that, and then it landed in the water!

"Oh no," Mark groaned. "I wish I'd stayed home with Mattie today." No fish, no berries, torn clothes, a bee sting, and to make matters worse, his hat was now floating in the middle of the pond!

Giving one last glance at his water-logged hat, Mark's mouth dropped open as he watched the biggest trout he'd ever seen leap into the air and snatch a bug that had been hovering over the water.

Lifting his arms in exasperation, Mark thought to himself, *I know Mattie's got to be having a better*

day at home than I am here, 'cause I'm sure having a
terrible day!

"We've got to find Ada!" Mattie shouted to Stella. "It looks like rain is coming, and if I don't find her before Mom gets home, I'll be in big trouble." Tears welled in Mattie's eyes and dribbled onto her cheeks. "W—what if I never see my little sister again? *Ach. . .* What a terrible day!"

"Calm down, Mattie, and take a deep breath." Stella put her arm around Mattie and gave her a reassuring squeeze. "Ada's got to be here someplace. Let's try and think if there's somewhere we haven't thought to look for her yet."

"I looked in the barn, and we've both looked all over the yard."

"Do you think she might have gone into the chicken coop?" Stella asked.

Mattie felt a sense of hope. "I don't know. Let's go see."

The girls ran to the chicken coop and checked it out, but Ada wasn't there.

"The only place we haven't looked is in the house and up the road." Mattie gulped. "I sure hope Ada didn't leave the yard. If she gets hit by a car. . ."

"Don't even think that." Stella motioned to the house. "Let's check there first, and if she's not in the house, then we'll go out on the road and search for her."

"Jah, okay." Mattie was glad her friend was with her

right now. Stella always seemed to be so calm about things, and that helped Mattie to relax a bit, too.

When they entered the house, all was quiet. If Ada was in here, she wasn't making a peep.

On the main floor of the house, Mattie and Stella looked in the kitchen, the living room, dining room, Mom and Dad's bedroom, and even the bathroom, but there was no sign of Ada.

"Let's go upstairs," Stella suggested. "Maybe Ada's in her bedroom."

Hope welled in Mattie's chest. She didn't know why she hadn't thought of that. If Ada had come into the house, she probably would go to her room to play.

Mattie dashed up the stairs and jerked open the door to Ada's bedroom. No sign of Ada in there—just lots of scattered toys on the floor. They even checked her closest, but she wasn't in there either.

"Let's look in all the other bedrooms," Stella said.

Mattie gave a nod. She didn't think Ada would have gone in any of the boys' rooms, but it was worth checking. However, after looking in each of those rooms they still hadn't found her.

"There's only one room left to check." Stella pointed to Mattie's bedroom. "If she's not in there, then I guess we'd better go back outside and start walking down the road."

Slowly, and with a feeling of dread, Mattie opened the door to her room. When she stepped inside she gasped. There lay Ada in the middle of Mattie's bed, with Mattie's favorite baby doll nestled in her arms.

Mattie might have been okay with that, but the doll had streaks of black ink all over its face!

"Just look what she did to my doll!" Mattie wailed. "Guess I should have gone fishing with Mark, 'cause I'm sure he's having a better time at the pond than I've had here on this terrible day!"

CHAPTER 6

The Grumpy Twins

That evening during supper, Mattie had a hard time
joining the conversation. She was still upset about the
way Ada had disappeared, and then the scribbling all
over her doll's face made it even worse. Mom had told
Mattie that she would try to get the ugly black stain off
with some cleanser, but Mattie was sure the doll was
ruined.

To make matters worse, the wind that had kicked up
earlier blew away all the pretty daisies Mattie had put
on the fence and porch railing. At least it hadn't rained
much, and it ended with a beautiful rainbow when the
sun came back out. But now Dad's folks, Grandma and
Grandpa Miller, were here, and they hadn't even seen
how nice Mattie had decorated everything. Grandma
said it didn't matter, that it was the thought that
counted. She also said she and Grandpa were just happy
to be here sharing a meal with them, but Mattie was still
disappointed. Nothing seemed to go right for her these
days, and now she felt really grumpy.

Mattie knew she should have been happy that

Grandma and Grandpa Miller could join them this evening. They lived on a small farm just outside of Walnut Creek, so they came by often to visit. Whenever Dad went over to see his parents, Mattie and Mark often went along. Grandma always had plenty of hugs to give, and usually had a batch of cookies in the oven. And somehow Grandpa always managed to have two packs of peppermint gum in his pocket—one for Mark and one for Mattie. When they arrived at their place, Grandpa, who was often in the barn, always came out to greet them, wearing a cheerful smile on his bearded face. The twins didn't hesitate to jump out of the buggy and race across the yard to see who could get to Grandpa first. Grandpa would usually tousle Mark's hair and tweak Mattie's nose. After that, he'd reach into his pants pocket and then hold out both hands, which were clamped tightly shut. Mark was usually the one who could guess which hand the gum was in.

Mattie glanced over at Mark, noticing his deep frown. She could tell that he felt grumpy, too, because he'd told her about everything he'd gone through while he was at the pond today. She was sure the bee sting must have hurt, and then losing all the berries he'd picked and not getting any fish had made it even worse. Not to mention the scratches he'd ended up with from all those prickly thorns.

"You two are awfully quiet this evening," Grandpa said, looking first at Mattie and then at Mark. "You're usually both so talkative."

Mattie shrugged her shoulders. Mark merely grunted.

"The twins had a rough day," Mom said, winking at Grandpa.

"What happened?" Grandma asked.

Mom looked at Mattie and then at Mark. "Why don't you take turns telling your stories?"

Mattie told about all the things that had gone wrong for her, and ended it by saying, "It was not a good day at all!"

Then Mark told about his misadventures at the pond. "Stupid bee sting still hurts," he added, holding up his sore hand. "And look at all the scratches I have on my arms."

"You two are quite a pair," Grandma said with a cluck of her tongue. "I'm sorry things went so poorly for you both today."

Grandpa gave a nod. "And I know from experience that a bee sting can really hurt."

"I concur," Mark said.

"What's that mean?" Mattie asked.

"It means 'I agree.'"

"Well, why didn't you just say that then?"

"I did."

"No, you didn't. You said, 'I concur.'"

"That's right, I do concur." Mark grinned as he looked over at Grandpa. "I learned that word from you, remember?"

Grandpa grinned and gave Mark's shoulder a squeeze. "Now back to the subject of bees. I remember once when I was a boy, I accidentally uncovered a bee's nest out in the woods." Deep wrinkles formed across his forehead as he slowly shook his head. "My face was so swollen from all those bee stings that my bruder, Sam, hardly recognized me when I ran home screaming that I'd been stung really bad."

"Were you allergic to the bee stings?" Ike asked.

"Nope. I just had so many on my face that it made me look really strange. It nearly scared my mamm half out of her wits."

"I can imagine," Mom said, nodding her head. "I'd be very concerned if one of my children came home looking like that."

Next, Dad told a story about the time he'd gotten stung trying to get a yellow jacket's nest out of the barn. "Guess everyone's been stung at least once in their life," he added with a chuckle.

"Not me," Mattie said. "I've never had a bee sting."

Grandpa patted Mattie's arm and said, "Well, your turn's coming, just you wait and see."

Mattie shuddered. She hoped Grandpa was wrong about that.

After supper, Dad said he thought they ought to make a batch of homemade ice cream.

"That's a good idea," Mom agreed. "I'll mix the ingredients, and then we'll set the ice cream freezer on the porch and everyone can take turns cranking the handle."

Dad gave a nod. "And no one had better argue about who gets to lick the wooden beaters this time, because

I've already decided that I get that honor tonight."

"Can you make strawberry ice cream?" Mattie asked. "That's my favorite."

"How about chocolate? That's my favorite kind," Mark said, smacking his lips.

"Strawberry's better," Mattie insisted. "It tastes *appenditlich*."

"Chocolate's delicious, too," Mark said.

Calvin, Russell, Ike, and even little Perry, all nodded. Mark knew they also liked chocolate, so he was sure that would be the kind Mom would make.

"Chocolate's good," Dad put in, "but I also like strawberry."

Grandma and Grandpa bobbed their heads in agreement. Ada nodded, too, but Mark was sure she was just copying Grandma and Grandpa, so her vote didn't really count.

"I'll tell you what I'm going to do," Mom said. "I'll make vanilla ice cream, and then I'll serve chocolate syrup and fresh strawberries to put over the top."

"Guess that'll be okay," Mark said, "but I don't like strawberries that well, so I'll only put chocolate topping on mine."

Mattie looked at Mark and wrinkled her nose. "I don't like chocolate that much, so I'm only going to put strawberries on mine."

Mark wrinkled his nose right back at her. "I wish you were more like me, Mattie."

"I wish you were more like me."

"You should both be happy being who you are,"

Grandma said. "God made each of you special."

"That's right," Grandpa agreed. "In Psalm 139:14, it says: 'I praise you because I am fearfully and wonderfully made.'"

"Does that mean Mattie and I are both unique?" Mark questioned.

"What's unique?" Mattie wanted to know. "Or do I have to get the dictionary and look it up?"

"It means you're both special and different," Grandpa said before Mark could respond.

"We're different alright," Mattie said. "I like dogs— Mark likes cats. I like collecting flowers—he collects rocks. I like to play baseball, and he doesn't care for the game."

"It's okay to be different," Grandma said. "You just need to enjoy each other's uniqueness and try to get along."

"That's right," Grandpa agreed. Then, looking over at Mark, he said, "Would you like to know another word for unique?"

"Jah, I sure would." Mark was always looking for new words to say, and since Grandpa liked using big words, too, he often taught them to Mark.

"Another word for unique is 'unequalled.' That means there's no one just like you."

"Unequalled," Mark repeated. "I like that word. Mattie and I are both unequalled."

Mattie frowned. "Oh great. Now he'll be saying 'un-equalled' all the time."

"I don't know about anyone else in this room, but I'd

like some ice cream before the evening runs out." Mom pushed her chair away from the table. "Mattie, if you'll help Grandma clear the dishes, I'll get the ingredients for the ice cream mixed up."

Mattie motioned to Mark. "What about him? What's he gonna do?"

"I'm going outside to feed my cat and see how her new busslin are doing," Mark said. He smiled at Grandma and Grandpa. "Lucky had her babies last night—and they're really cute."

"How many did she have?" Grandma asked.

"Five in all."

"That's great," Grandpa said. "Before we head home tonight, we'll have to go out to the barn and take a look."

"In the meantime, while Calvin and Russell gather the ice and rock salt, I'm going to get the ice cream freezer out of the storage shed," Dad said.

"What's Ike gonna do?" Mark wanted to know.

"I'm going out to the barn to groom my horse so he looks good when I take him to the young people's singing on Sunday night."

"Are you takin' your *aldi* to the singing?" Mattie asked.

Ike tweaked the end of Mattie's nose. "You're not supposed to ask questions about my girlfriend, little sister."

Mattie giggled. Mark rolled his eyes. Everyone else just smiled.

"Well, let's get with it!" Dad clapped his hands. "If we don't get busy now it'll be time to go to bed, and then nobody will get any ice cream."

Everyone hurried off to do their jobs, until a little later, when it was just about dark, Dad called them to the porch to take turns cranking the handle of the ice cream freezer. Mark and Mattie went first, because they weren't as strong as their older brothers, and as the ice cream began to freeze up, it became harder to crank.

"Let's go out in the yard and look at the stars," Mark said to Mattie after they'd both taken their turns cranking the handle. He glanced toward the west, where the sun was below the horizon. All that was left of daylight was the faint orange glow of the beautiful sunset they'd seen just minutes earlier.

"Okay, let's go." Mattie hurried into the yard, and Mark followed.

"Look up there," Mark said, pointing to the twinkling stars overhead. "See. . .there's the Big Dipper!"

"And there's the Little Dipper. I'll bet there must be hundreds of stars," Mattie said.

"Nope. There's more than that."

"Thousands?"

Mark shook his head. "There are about 100 billion stars in our galaxy."

"Wow, that's amazing! How do you know so much about the stars?"

"I read a book about them at the library. You could learn a lot if you read more, too."

"The kind of books you read are boring," Mattie said.

"No, they're not."

"Jah, they are."

"No, they. . ."

"Mattie! Mark! Come inside now, the ice cream's ready!" Mom called.

"First one to the porch gets the first taste of ice cream!" Mark hollered. The day might not have started out so good, but he was glad it had ended well. Maybe, just maybe, Dad would give in and let him lick the beaters. That is, if Mattie didn't think to ask first.

CHAPTER 7

First Day of School

Mattie knelt on the grass in front of the pond and stared at her reflection. She noticed that her black head covering was on crooked, so she reached up to straighten it. When she glanced at the water again, her reflection was gone and another had taken its place. It was Mark looking back at her now. What was he doing at the pond? She thought she'd come here alone today.

Mattie turned, but there was no sign of Mark behind her. She looked back at the water and saw her own reflection again. Maybe she'd just imagined seeing Mark's reflection.

Bzzz. . . Bzzz. . . A bee buzzed overhead. She swatted at it, and then quickly jerked her hand away, so she wouldn't get stung.

"Everyone gets stung sometime," she heard Grandpa say.

"No, no. . . Not me!"

Mattie stared into the water and gasped when she saw Mark's reflection once more. What was going on? Was he playing another one of his silly tricks on her?

She whirled around quickly, thinking she'd catch him this time, but Mark wasn't there—only the buzzing bee overhead. *Bzzz. . . Bzzz. . . Bzzz. . .* The buzzing kept on.

Mattie scrambled to her feet and tried to run, but she couldn't move. Her feet felt like they were stuck in a bucket of cement.

"Help me! Help me!" she cried. "I can't move, and there's a bee after me!"

"Mattie. . ." Someone was calling to her, but their voice sounded far away.

Mark, is that you? Mattie tried to speak, but she couldn't seem to get the words out of her mouth. All she could do was moan.

Someone touched Mattie's arm and gave it a shake. "Mattie, wake up."

Feeling as if she were being pulled from a fog, Mattie opened one eye, and then the other. Mark stared down at her with a peculiar look on his face. "It's time to get up," he said. "Didn't you hear your alarm clock buzzing? I could hear it clear out in the hall."

Mattie rolled over and hit the button on the clock by her bed. "Oh, the buzzing I heard must have been in my dream," she murmured. "I—I thought it was a bee."

"Huh? What were you dreaming about?"

"I was dreaming that I saw my reflection in the pond, and then I saw. . . Oh, never mind." Mattie figured if she told Mark about her dream, he'd probably think it was weird and tease her again.

"Hurry up and get out of bed," Mark said. "We start

back to school today. Did you forget?"

Mattie groaned and pulled the covers over her head. "No, but I wish I could."

"What was that?"

She lowered the covers just a bit. "Nothing. Go on downstairs, and tell Mom I'll be there as soon as I get dressed."

"Okay." Mark practically skipped out of the room. He looked excited this morning. He was probably glad they were going to school. Well, Mattie wasn't glad. She always dreaded the first day of school and wished she could think of some way to get out of going. She realized, though, that if she didn't go to school today, then tomorrow would be her first day of school. So she might as well get up, get ready, and get this day over with—unless she could convince Mom to let her stay home. Maybe she wouldn't have to go to school any days this week.

When Mattie entered the kitchen a short time later, she found Mom standing in front of the counter, putting sandwiches in everyone's lunch boxes.

"Guder mariye, schlofkopp," Mom said, looking over her shoulder at Mattie.

"Good morning," Mattie mumbled, slouching against the table. She really felt like a sleepyhead.

"What's wrong? Did you get up on the wrong side of the bed?" Mom asked.

"No, I. . .uh. . .think I need to stay home from school

today—and maybe all week."

Mom's eyebrows shot up. "What's wrong, Mattie? Are you *grank*?"

Mattie didn't want to lie and say she was sick, but she had to do something to keep from going to school. "I'm. . .uh. . .feeling a little under the weather." She'd heard Grandpa Troyer say that when he wasn't feeling his best. Maybe by saying that now, it would be enough for Mom to let her stay home today.

Mom stopped what she was doing, hurried over to Mattie, and touched her forehead. "You don't seem to have a fever. Open your mouth and let me take a look at your throat."

Mattie did as Mom asked. This wasn't working out so well. She was sure there was nothing wrong with her throat, and Mom would know that just as soon as she looked.

"I don't see any unusual redness," Mom said. "Does your stomach hurt?"

Mattie shook her head. "Uh. . .no, not really, but. . ."

"Then I don't think you're sick." Mom gave Mattie's shoulder a little squeeze. "Now hurry and set the table so we can eat." She looked over at Mark, who stood near the sink smiling from ear to ear. He obviously knew Mattie had been trying to get out of going to school. Mom probably did, too.

"Well, I don't know about anyone else, but I'm hungerich," Mark said. "And the sooner we eat, the sooner we can leave for school."

"Jah, I can hardly wait," Mattie mumbled under her breath.

Mom pointed at Mark's feet. "How come you're wearing two different shoes this morning?"

Mark's face turned red as a radish as he stared down at his feet. "Oh, I. . .uh. . .guess I was so excited to get dressed and head for school that I wasn't paying attention to which shoes I was putting on my feet."

Mattie stifled a giggle. On one foot Mark wore a black sneaker. On the other foot he wore one of his black dress shoes. How in the world could he not have known what he was doing? Mark must have been really mixed up this morning.

Mom chuckled and patted Mark's shoulder. "Well, hurry upstairs and exchange your dress shoe with your other sneaker so we can eat. I hear your daed and the older boys coming up the back steps now, so I'm sure they'll expect breakfast to be on the table."

"I'm going right now." Mark hurried from the room and Mattie began setting the table. It was obvious that she wasn't going to get out of attending school today. All she could do was grin and bear it.

As Mark and Mattie headed to school that morning, Mark felt like singing and kicking up his heels. Instead, he just swung his lunch pail back and forth as he hurried up the dirt path. He was excited about going to school because he enjoyed learning new things. He especially liked learning new words. Of course, sometimes he used big, long words that even his teacher didn't understand. And whether he'd either heard them from Grandpa Miller or found them in the dictionary, he always made sure he knew what they meant before he tried using them in a sentence.

"What are you thinking about?" Mattie asked, bumping Mark's arm.

"School."

"Me, too. Sure wish I was older and had already graduated from the eighth grade." Mattie looked at Calvin and Russell riding their bikes up ahead. They'd both saved up some of the money they'd earned selling produce at their roadside stand this summer and had bought their own bikes. That's why they got to ride to school and Mark and Mattie had to walk. "This is Russell's last year at school, and Calvin only has two more years after this one," she said.

"That's right, and we won't be far behind them." Mark smiled. "So we need to study hard and learn all we can."

"That's easy for you to say. You're so *schmaert*, and you always get good grades."

"You'd be smart, too, if you'd quit daydreaming so much and start paying attention to what the teacher says."

"I do pay attention. I just can't remember well."

"You'd remember more if you didn't think about other things all the time."

"I can't help it," she said. "Things just seem to pop into my head."

"Well, remember this—you're 'unequalled,' so you can do anything you want to do."

Mattie said nothing, so Mark shrugged his shoulders and kept walking toward the schoolhouse. His legs couldn't seem to move fast enough, he was so eager to get there. He didn't understand Mattie's daydreaming, and didn't think he'd ever figure her out. Sometimes he wished he had a twin brother instead of a dreamy-eyed sister who was nothing like him at all. But then if they were just alike, that would probably be boring.

When Mark and Mattie entered the schoolyard, Mattie spotted Stella talking with a group of girls over by the swings, so she decided to join them while Mark went to visit with some of the boys.

Even though Mattie didn't like all the schoolwork she knew she'd have to do, she did enjoy getting to see all her friends. It was fun to talk about the things they'd done over the summer months. Some, like Becky Yoder, had gone on a trip to visit family who lived in another state. Mattie wished she had relatives living somewhere other than Ohio. It would be fun to ride the bus or train and visit somewhere she hadn't been before. But at least they got to ride in their driver's van whenever they visited Grandpa and Grandma Troyer in Burton. That was better than staying home all the time.

Mattie said hello to Stella and the other girls, and then someone suggested they take turns pushing some of the younger ones on the swings. Mattie didn't want to do that, so she picked some pretty flowers growing in the field next to the schoolhouse to give to their teacher, Anna Ruth. She'd only picked a few flowers when the school bell rang.

Mattie sighed and shuffled into the schoolhouse behind the other children. Like it or not, her school day was about to begin.

When Mattie and the others entered the schoolhouse, the boys jostled one another as they hung their straw hats on some hooks on the wall, and then put their lunch boxes away on a bench at the back of the room. On the girls' side of the room things were a little quieter, as they found places for their lunch boxes as well. Then Mattie hurried to the front of the room, where the teacher's desk sat in the corner, and gave her the flowers she'd picked.

"Why, thank you, Mattie. These are lovely, and it was nice of you to think of me." When Anna Ruth smiled, the whole room seemed to light up. She had light brown hair, hazel-colored eyes, and a pretty face. Mattie was surprised the twenty-year-old schoolteacher wasn't married yet. In fact, as far as she knew, Anna Ruth didn't even have a boyfriend. Maybe she, like Mattie, didn't plan to get married. Or maybe she just hadn't found the right fellow yet.

"I'm glad you like the flowers, and you're welcome," Mattie said before taking her seat. Maybe she would do better in school this year if she stayed on the good side of their teacher.

"Good morning, boys and girls," Anna Ruth said after the scholars had all taken their seats.

"Good morning, Anna Ruth," the children replied.

Next, the teacher read a verse of scripture from the Bible. " 'If any of you lacks wisdom, you should ask God.' James 1:5."

Mattie felt like hiding under her desk. Had Anna Ruth chosen that verse to read this morning because she knew Mattie wasn't smart? Well, why wouldn't she know it? Mattie had struggled in school last year, and unless God gave her a good dose of wisdom soon, she'd probably struggle this year, too.

Dear God, she silently prayed, *help me to be smart like Mark.*

Next, it was time to stand with the others and recite the Lord's Prayer. When that was done, everyone filed to the front of the room to sing a few songs. The first song they sang was called, "Sing Little Children, Sing," but Mattie had a hard time concentrating on the words. It was easier to look out the window, where a stream of light filtered through and drifted across the light-colored walls and dark wooden floor. She spotted a big old horsefly on the window, buzzing angrily and trying to find its way out. She was tempted to leave her place and open the window so the fly could escape, but figured she'd be in trouble with the teacher if she did that. Well, at least that old fly hadn't gotten trapped on the flypaper hanging from the wall in one corner of the room. Maybe when the door was opened at recess the fly would find its way outside to freedom.

Glancing out the window next to it, Mattie noticed a herd of black-and-white cows grazing and swishing their tails in the pasture across the way. Out another window on the other side of the room, she saw a field of dreary-looking dried cornstalks. Summer was almost over; there was no doubt about it. Soon the warm days of August would turn cool, and autumn would swoop right in. Mattie dreaded walking to school when the weather was cold or rainy. One more reason she hoped for a new bike that would get her to and from school a lot quicker than walking.

Mattie's mind snapped to attention when Stella poked her arm and whispered, "It's time to take our seats again."

Mattie shuffled back to her desk and sat down, dreading the arithmetic lesson she knew would be coming next. Later in the day, they would study reading and spelling. Mattie wasn't looking forward to those subjects either. She glanced up at the sign on the wall above the teacher's desk: YOU ARE RESPONSIBLE FOR YOU. It was a reminder that she needed to study harder to get good grades, but sometimes her thoughts took her in other directions.

As the morning wore on, Mattie's stomach began to rumble. She glanced at the battery-operated clock on the wall and smiled when she saw that it was almost time for lunch.

After lunch, some of the older students got a game of baseball going. Mark didn't want to play, but after his friend John Schrock, who was Stella's cousin, kept pestering him about it, he finally agreed.

"It'll be fun," John said, as he and Mark waited to take their turn up to bat.

"We'll see about that," Mark muttered. It might be

fun for those who could play well, but he didn't like baseball and had never been able to play the game without messing up. Mattie, on the other hand, played baseball as well as any of the boys. Everyone wanted Mattie on their team. In fact, when it was her turn to bat, he could see the look of happiness on her face. If Mattie did even half as well in school as she did on the ball field, she'd be an excellent student.

The first ball that was pitched came right over home plate. Mattie swung and—*crack!*—the bat hit the ball with such force that it sailed right over the pitcher's head and landed in the neighbor's field of drying corn.

Everyone cheered as Mattie ran around all the bases and made a home run. Russell and Calvin even whistled real loud.

"Good going!" Stella patted Mattie on the back. "I'm sure glad you're on our team."

"*Danki*," Mattie said with a grin. Her cheeks were rosy, and her blue eyes sparkled like twinkling fireflies on a hot summer night. It was obvious that she enjoyed playing ball very much.

Mark was glad his twin sister had made a home run, but oh, how he wished he could play as well as she did. Mattie made that home run look as easy as pie. It just wasn't right that a girl could play better than her brother.

John was up to bat next, and he hit a ball that took him to second base.

Then it was Aaron Stutzman's turn. He hit the ball on the second swing, and it took him to first base, while

John ran quickly and made it to third base.

"It's your turn now," Mattie said, smiling at Mark. Did she know how nervous he felt?

Mark's palms grew sweaty as he stepped up to home plate and grabbed the wooden bat. Then, squinting against the glare of the sun, he positioned the bat over his shoulder.

The first pitch flew past Mark and hit the fence.

"Strike one!" someone hollered.

The catcher quickly recovered the ball and threw it back to the pitcher.

The pitcher threw the ball again, and when it blurred toward home plate, Mark swung with all his might. But he missed the ball, lost his balance, and fell on his back with a groan.

The girls gasped, and several of the boys laughed. Mark wasn't hurt, but he sure was embarrassed. He couldn't believe what had just happened to him.

Gritting his teeth, Mark clambered to his feet, and more determined than ever, he gripped the bat once again. As he waited for the next pitch, he whispered a little prayer. *Help me to hit this ball, Lord.*

Whack! This time he hit the ball with such force that it sailed through the air, just missing the pitcher's head.

Mark felt pretty good about that, but he only made it halfway to first base when he got tagged out. That was the trouble when you couldn't run fast.

"Hey, brainiac with the carrot top hair," Aaron Stutzman jeered, "looks like you can't run any better than you can hit! Maybe you should let your twin sister fill in for you the next time you're up to bat."

Mattie planted both hands on her hips and glared at Aaron. "You shouldn't make fun of my bruder or call him names."

"She's right," Russell called from the sidelines where he'd been watching. "Mark just needs more time to practice."

Mark's face heated, and he knew it had turned red. It was bad enough that he couldn't play well, did his sister and brother have to embarrass him in front of the others by sticking up for him like that? This was not a good way to begin the new school year, and as he walked off the ball field he decided that from now on he'd find something else to do during recess.

CHAPTER 8

Poor Twinkles

"Sure wish I hadn't played ball during lunch recess today," Mark told Mattie on the way home from school. "I don't like playing ball, and I don't like people laughing at me or sticking up for me when I mess up. If the teacher doesn't mind, I'm not gonna play that game anymore."

"What Russell said was right, you know. You just need to practice more," Mattie said. "Mom always says that practice makes perfect."

"I might practice if I liked playing ball, but I don't, so what's the point in practicing?" He nudged Mattie's arm. "What about you? If you practiced spelling more you might be good at that, too."

Mattie's cheeks turned pink. "You know I don't like spelling, and I don't want to talk about this anymore!" She ran quickly ahead of him.

That was fine with Mark. With the way he felt about the baseball game, he'd rather walk by himself anyway.

Trudging along with his head down and shoulders slumped, he stopped to dig the toe of his boot into the dirt. When he spotted a ground beetle moving slowly through the dirt, he squatted down and studied it for a few seconds. Ground beetles were often found under rocks, twigs, or tree stumps, and they were big and black. Burying beetles were another type of interesting bug, but they had spots on their backs, kind of like ladybugs. Beetles, spiders, grasshoppers, and other insects didn't bother Mark at all, but he sure didn't like snakes. In fact, he disliked snakes even more than he disliked Mattie's yappy little dog.

"Hey Mark, what are ya lookin' at?" Aaron Stutzman called as he walked up behind Mark and tapped his shoulder.

"Nothin' much," Mark mumbled. "Just watchin' a big fat beetle."

"Well, if ya watched the ball as hard as you're starin' at that bug, ya might be able to hit better." Aaron snickered. "Maybe you should get your twin sister to teach you how to run faster, too."

Mark clenched his fingers so tightly that his nails dug into the palms of his hands. He didn't need the reminder that Mattie could play ball better and run faster than he could, and he was relieved when Aaron went on his way.

Farther down the road, Mark found a flat rock with red stripes running through it, so he stuck it in his pocket. It would look good with some of the other unusual rocks he'd collected and put in a glass jar in his room. Then he rose to his feet and continued his walk toward home. He was almost there when he spotted a teenage boy riding up the road on his fancy black-and-silver bicycle. Oh, how he wished he had a bike like that. If he'd been riding a bike instead of walking he could have pedaled right on past Aaron when he'd started making fun of him. And if he had a bike, that would get him home really quickly like his brothers Russell and Calvin.

When Mark entered his yard a short time later, he saw Mattie on the grass playing with Twinkles.

"Sit, Twinkles! Sit!" Mattie snapped her fingers and pointed to the mutt.

Woof! Woof! Instead of sitting, Twinkles darted across the lawn and nipped at Mark's pant leg.

"Get away from me, you annoying *hund*!" Mark shouted. He was in no mood for this today. "Go find someone else to pester."

"Don't be nasty to my dog. Twinkles only wants you to pet her," Mattie said.

"Well, she has a funny way of showing it," Mark grumbled.

"You know something?"

"What's that?"

"Twinkles is a good dog, and she doesn't nip at anyone but you." Mattie frowned. "I think it's because she knows you don't like her."

Mark bobbed his head. "She's right about that, and I don't feel like petting her right now."

"I'm going inside to see if Mom will fix me a snack." Mattie turned and hurried into the house.

Woof! Woof! Twinkles nipped at Mark's pant leg

again, this time tearing a small hole in it.

"That's it! You're going in your dog pen!" Mark bent down, scooped Twinkles into his arms, and marched over to the dog pen. After he'd put Twinkles inside, he slammed the gate shut with a bang. "There, that oughta teach you for ripping my pants!"

When Mark entered the house, he found Mattie and Mom sitting at the kitchen table eating cheese and apple slices, and they each had a glass of milk.

"Wash your hands, and have a seat at the table," Mom said, motioning to an empty chair. "Mattie's been telling me about her first day back at school, and I'd like to hear how your day went, too."

Mark grunted. "It was baremlich."

"Why was it terrible?" Mom asked, raising her eyebrows.

Mark washed his hands and took a seat at the table; then he told Mom all about his day.

"I'm sorry." Mom ruffled Mark's hair. "I'm sure tomorrow will go better, and don't worry about your pants. I'll see that the tear's mended."

"Sure wish we didn't have to play ball at school. Wish we could just stay inside and learn new words," Mark said, reaching for an apple slice and a piece of cheese.

"Learning is good for your mind," Mom said, "but your body needs exercise, too."

"That's right," Mattie agreed. "And playing ball is good exercise."

"So's riding a bike." Mark looked at Mom and smiled. "If I had a bike I could get places quicker, and it would be good exercise to help strengthen my legs. If I had a bike I could run some errands for you, too."

Mom said nothing, just gave a little nod. Did that mean she was thinking about it? Was it possible that he'd get a new bike for his birthday? He sure hoped so, because besides how wonderful it would be if Grandpa and Grandma Troyer could come to his and Mattie's party, a new bike was the only gift he really wanted this year.

"I'm done with my snack now," Mattie said, setting her empty glass on the table. "Is it okay if I go outside and play?"

Mom nodded. "Just be sure to change out of your school dress first."

Mattie took her dishes to the sink and hurried from the room.

"I'm going to get Ada and Perry up from their afternoon nap," Mom said to Mark. "After you're done with your snack, be sure to clear away your dishes."

"Okay."

While Mark enjoyed his snack, he began to feel a bit better. Maybe Mom was right. Tomorrow might go better at school. Maybe he could talk the teacher into letting him do something else while the others played ball during recess.

Mark heard the back door open and close, and figured Mattie must have gone outside. A few minutes later the door opened and closed again. Then Mattie stomped into the kitchen, and with her hands on her hips, she frowned at Mark. "Did you put Twinkles in her pen?"

"Jah."

"How come?"

" 'Cause I was tired of her nipping at my pant leg."

"But you came inside for a snack, so how could she have bothered you then?"

"She would have bothered me when I went back outside."

"Well, Twinkles is my dog, and I'd appreciate it if you'd let me put her in the pen." Mattie left the kitchen and went out the back door.

Mark took his time eating his snack. When he was done, he put his dishes in the sink and went to his room to change his clothes. Maybe he'd lie on his bed awhile and study his spelling words for tomorrow. Better yet, he could take the words out to the barn, and after he'd studied he would play with Lucky and her new kittens.

Mattie spent the next half hour playing with Twinkles and trying to teach her to jump through a hoop. Today for some reason Twinkles was being a stubborn dog and didn't want to learn anything new, so Mattie finally gave up and went back to the house. She figured she might as well study her spelling words for a bit.

When Mattie entered the house she took a peek in the kitchen to see if Mark was still there, but the room was empty so she figured he must be upstairs in his bedroom.

Mattie went up the steps and into her own room. Then, with a big yawn, she curled up on her bed with the list of spelling words their teacher had given them today. "Camping. . .fishing. . .fuzzy. . ." Mattie's voice trailed off as her eyes became heavy, and soon she drifted off to sleep.

Woof! Woof! Woof!

Mattie's eyes popped open, and she jumped off the bed. Hurrying over to the window, she pulled the curtains aside and looked out. She saw Mark in the yard, doing something with Twinkles.

Woof! Woof! Twinkles raced back and forth, barking and leaping into the air.

Mattie rushed out of the room, raced down the stairs, and out the back door.

When she stepped into the yard, she halted. Mark had an old rag in his hand, and he was pulling on it as Twinkles tugged on the other end.

"Absatz!" Mattie hollered. "You're gonna make my dog tired, doin' that!"

"I'm not hurtin' her," Mark said. "I'm tryin' to pay Twinkles some attention like you asked me to do before, and she seems to like my teasing."

Mattie wasn't sure what to do or say about that. Twinkles did seem to be having a good time. "Would you like to help me teach Twinkles a new trick?"

Mark shrugged. "Sure, why not?"

CHAPTER 9

Creepy Things

For the rest of the afternoon, and even as they sat at the table eating supper that evening, Mattie thought about her plan to show Mark that she could tease, too. Remembering that Mark didn't like snakes, Mattie had borrowed a rubber snake from Calvin, who liked to collect creepy things. Then when Mark was outside feeding his cat, she'd snuck into his room and put the snake under the top sheet in his bed. She stifled a snicker, imagining the look of shock on Mark's face when he pulled the covers back and got ready to crawl into bed tonight. Since Mark was afraid of snakes of all kinds, he'd probably think it was a real snake and be scared silly.

"That was a very good meal," Dad said, patting his stomach before pushing his chair away from the table. He grinned over at Mom. "Fried chicken has always been my favorite meal, Alice."

She smiled in return. "I'm glad you enjoyed it, Willard."

"So now everyone needs to get their evening chores

done," Dad said as he moved toward the door. "Then we'll all gather in the living room to read from the Bible before we go to bed."

"Mattie and Mark, I'd like you both to do the dishes." Mom motioned to the sink. "After that, you'll need to take out the garbage."

"I don't mind taking out the garbage"—Mark frowned—"but do I have to do the dishes?"

"Jah, you do," Mom said. "I'm going to give the little ones their baths, and the older boys have some chores to help your daed with in the barn, so I need both of you to help in the kitchen."

Mark groaned. Mattie sighed. She didn't want to do anything with Mark this evening. In fact, she thought it would be better if she could do the dishes alone.

"Can't Mark take out the garbage while I do the dishes?" she asked.

Mom shook her head. "The dishes need to be washed and dried, and I think it's good if you and Mark learn how to work together. Besides, you'll get the job done much quicker if one of you washes and the other one dries."

"Well, let's get this over with then," Mark said, sliding his chair away from the table.

Mattie helped Mom clear the dishes while Mark filled the sink with soap and water. Then Mom sent Perry to his room to get his pajamas while she gave Ada a bath.

"Do you want to wash or dry?" Mattie asked Mark.

He shrugged. "Makes no difference to me, 'cause

either one is just as bad."

"Fine then. I'll wash and you can dry."

"I've changed my mind," Mark said. "It does make a difference, and I'd rather wash and you can dry."

Mattie shook her head determinedly. "It's already been decided. I'm gonna wash and you're gonna dry."

"Who made you the boss?" He squinted his eyes into tiny slits.

"Didn't say I was the boss, but you already said it makes no difference, and I want to wash the dishes, so you'll have to dry."

Mark turned his hands palms-up. "Oh, all right."

Mattie stepped up to the sink and plunged her hands into the soapy water. Then she sloshed the sponge over the plates, making sure they were clean. Finally, she rinsed them well before putting them in the dish drainer for Mark to dry.

"You'll have to do this one over again." Mark plunked one of the plates back into the soapy water. "It's despicable."

"Despica-what?" Mattie asked.

"Despicable."

"What's that mean?"

"It means the dish is terrible, because it's dirty."

Mattie flicked some soapy water at her brother. She was getting tired of him using big words.

By the time Mattie and Mark finished the dishes, she was frustrated with him. It seemed like every other dish she washed he said was despicable and asked her to wash it again. The next time they did the dishes together he could wash and she would dry!

"Guess we'd better take out the garbage now," Mark said after he'd hung up the dish towel. "I'll take this one and you can take the other." He pointed to the two bags of garbage sitting near the back door.

Mattie was tempted to argue about which bag she would take, but decided that it didn't really matter. She just wanted to get the job done so she could do something fun before going to bed.

When they stepped outside and headed for the garbage cans behind the barn, Mattie's nose twitched. "There's a skunk somewhere nearby, and it really stinks."

"Aw, you're probably just smelling the garbage," Mark said.

"No, it's not that. I know the difference between garbage smell and skunk smell."

As they drew closer to the garbage cans, the smell became stronger. "Hurry up, Mark. Get your bag of garbage put in the can, and let's get back to the house before we get sprayed by that stinky skunk."

Mark tossed his bag of garbage into the can and took off for the house. Mattie was right behind him. As they stepped onto the porch, Mattie turned and saw a skunk with its tail in the air parade right through their yard. She dashed into the house behind Mark and quickly shut the door.

"Whew, that was close!"

Mark gave a nod. "I'm sure glad we didn't get sprayed."

Just then Dad called from the living room, "Mattie. . .

Mark. . . It's time to read the Bible now."

"As soon as we wash our hands we'll be right there," Mattie said. She'd almost forgotten about the Bible reading time.

When Mattie and Mark entered the living room, Mom and Dad were seated on the sofa with Perry and Ada between them. Calvin, Russell, and Ike had taken seats in the overstuffed chairs, so Mark and Mattie had to sit on the floor.

Dad was just getting ready to read from the Bible, when Calvin pointed to the window. "What's that on the curtain? Looks like something dark."

Everyone's attention went to the window. With only the light from the two gas lanterns in the room, it was kind of hard to see.

"That looks like a bat!" Mom shrieked. "Someone, quick, get a bucket or a box. We need something to catch that critter in!"

"I'll go out to the porch to get the bucket I've used to put fish in," Russell said.

Dad gave a nod. "That's a good idea. Now, everyone else, stay put. We don't want anyone getting bit by the flying rodent because it could carry rabies."

Russell raced out of the room, and Dad walked over to the other side of the room where the windows were located, then he slowly approached the curtain from the side. So far, the bat didn't seem to know he was there.

"Be careful, Willard," Mom warned, while keeping her arms around Ada and Perry.

Mattie held her breath as Dad took the curtain

and quickly, but gently, folded it over the bat to hold it in place. When Russell came running back in, Dad shook the bat into the bucket; then hurriedly placed a magazine over the opening so the bat couldn't fly out.

"Whew, that was too close!" Mattie sighed, expelling air.

"That little brown *genus myotis* was kinda cute," Mark said as they all watched Russell take the bat out the front door. "He must have flown in the back door when Mattie and I took the garbage out, 'cause I think we left it open."

"*Genus myotis*? Does that mean bat?" Calvin asked.

Mark bobbed his head. "Jah. It means 'mouse-eared bat,' which is one of the most common bats around. They like to eat moths, wasps, beetles, and mosquitoes, among other things. Oh, and I read once that most bats don't even have rabies, so we probably could have looked at it closer before Russell took the critter outside."

Mattie couldn't believe how much her twin brother knew about bats. Of course, he knew a lot about many things because he liked to read so much.

"Even so, you can't take any chances when it comes to a wild animal, so it's better to be safe," Dad said. "You could get mighty sick if you got bit and contracted rabies, and the treatment for rabies can be pretty painful, too."

Once the excitement calmed down, everyone settled in and got comfortable again while Dad prepared to read.

"Tonight I'll be reading from Luke 6:31," Dad said as he opened the big leather Bible. " 'Do to others as you would have them do to you.' "

Mattie thought about the surprise waiting for Mark in his bed. God's Word said she should do to others as she would have them do to her. She wouldn't want someone to put something she was afraid of in her bed. She realized now that what she'd done was wrong. Besides, with the bat incident, she thought they'd had enough scaring for one night. Somehow she had to sneak into Mark's room before he went up there, and get that creepy rubber snake out of his bed.

Day of Surprises

Mark stepped into his bedroom, yawned, and stretched his arms over his head. Today had been long and tiring, and he was more than ready for bed. Smelling that skunk, and then the little brown bat in the living room had sure livened things up this evening.

After putting on his pajamas, he knelt on the floor by his bed to say his prayers.

Dear Lord: Bless my family, and keep us all safe tonight. Be with Grandpa and Grandma Miller, and help Grandpa Troyer to feel better so he and Grandma can come to Mattie's and my birthday party next week. Thank You for not letting anyone get hurt by the bat. Oh, and please help me and Mattie to do well on our spelling test tomorrow. Amen.

Mark stood, pulled his covers aside, and let out a yelp. There was an ugly-looking snake curled up in his bed!

He dashed across the room, jerked open his

bedroom door, and ran into the hall.

"*Schlang!* Schlang!" Mark hollered when he bumped into Mattie, who'd just come up the stairs. "There's a schlang in my bed!"

Mattie grabbed hold of Mark's arm and gave it a little shake. "Calm down. It's not a real snake."

"It—it sure looks real." Mark's heart was beating so fast he could hardly get his breath.

She shook her head. "Well, it's not. It's just a rubber snake."

"H–how do you know that?"

"Because I put it there," she whispered.

"What was that?"

"I borrowed the snake from Calvin and put it in your bed."

Mark's forehead wrinkled. "Why would you do a thing like that?"

"Well, you're always teasing others, and I wanted to show you that I could tease, too." Mattie stared at the floor. "After Dad read the Bible verse to us this evening, I realized what I'd done was wrong. So I was heading to your room to get the snake, but you got there first." She lifted her gaze to look at him. "I'm sorry, Mark. Will you forgive me?"

Mark tapped his bare foot and stared at Mattie. She really did look sorry. "I'll forgive you, but you'd better never do anything like that again."

"I promise I won't."

Clomp! Clomp! Clomp!

Mark turned and saw Dad coming up the stairs. "I

thought you two were getting ready for bed," he said.

Mark knew if he didn't think of something quick, he and Mattie would both be in trouble. "Oh, uh. . .Mattie and I were just talking about something, but we're ready for bed." He looked at Mattie again and noticed she wasn't wearing her nightgown. "Well, at least I'm ready for bed."

"I'm going to my room right now," Mattie said.

"All right then. Sleep well, you two." Dad gave them both a hug and clomped back down the stairs.

Mattie started for her room, but Mark grabbed hold of her arm. "Wait a minute. Isn't there something you forgot?"

She shook her head. "I can't think of anything."

He pointed to his bedroom door. "You'd better get that snake out of my bed or I'm gonna tell Dad what you did."

"Can't you take it out yourself? It's just a rubber one, you know."

"I don't care. You're the one who put it in my bed, so you're the one who should take it out." Truth was, even though the snake was only rubber, it looked real, and Mark didn't want to touch it. He could tolerate a lot of other things, but not creepy snakes—not even a rubber one!

Mattie hesitated a minute, and finally nodded. "Okay. Since Calvin's already in bed, I'll put the snake in my laundry basket and give it to him in the morning."

"I don't care where you put it, just as long as it's not in my room!"

When Mattie woke up the next morning she looked at the clock and realized she'd forgotten to set her alarm the night before. If she didn't move quickly, she'd either miss breakfast or be late for school. She hurried to get dressed, ran down the hall to the bathroom to wash her face and brush her teeth, and then raced down the stairs.

"You should have been down here sooner," Mom scolded when Mattie entered the kitchen. "You'd better hurry and eat your cereal or you'll be late for school."

"I know, and I'll hurry." Mattie noticed that there was no one else at the table.

"Where is everyone?" she asked.

"The little ones are still in bed, your daed and Ike left for work, and your brothers are on their way to school," Mom said.

"Even Mark?"

Mom shook her head. "He's in the barn with Lucky and her busslin, but you'd better hurry and eat so the two of you won't be late."

"Okay." Mattie picked up her spoon. Then, remembering that she needed to pray, she bowed her head. *Dear Lord, help today to be a good day; thank You for this food; keep us all safe, and help the days go quickly until Mark's and my birthday.*

When Mattie opened her eyes, Mom tapped her shoulder. "I'm going upstairs to gather everyone's dirty laundry, because I need to wash clothes today. Oh, and

Mattie, don't forget to put Twinkles in her pen before you leave for school."

"I'll do it, Mom," Mattie said around a mouthful of cereal.

Mom left the room and went up the stairs. A few minutes later, Mattie heard a terrible scream. "Schlang! Schlang!"

Oh no! Mattie gulped. She'd forgotten to put the rubber snake back in Calvin's room this morning.

Mattie left her seat and raced up the stairs. She found Mom in her bedroom, staring at the snake in the laundry basket and looking pale as a bucket of goat's milk.

"It's okay, Mom. It's not real. It's just a rubber snake," Mattie quickly said. It was obvious that Mom didn't care for snakes any more than Mark did.

"B–but how did it get in your laundry basket?" Mom sputtered.

"Well, I. . .uh. . .borrowed it from Calvin."

Mom's eyebrows furrowed. "How come?"

Mattie wasn't sure what to say. She didn't want to lie about it, but wasn't sure she should tell Mom that she'd put the snake in Mark's bed. Mom would probably scold her for that.

Mom's forehead wrinkled as she stared at Mattie with a questioning look. "What's going on, Mattie? Why did you borrow Calvin's rubber snake?"

"Well, I. . .uh. . ." Tears welled in Mattie's eyes, then she blurted out the whole story, knowing she would feel much better once she'd told the truth.

"Oh Mattie, you know it's not right to tease someone

like that—especially with something you know they're afraid of," Mom said, slowly shaking her head.

Mattie nodded. "I told Mark I was sorry and I was going to put the snake back in Calvin's room this morning, but I forgot." She clasped Mom's hand. "I'm sorry the schlang scared you, and I promise I won't do anything like that ever again."

"I'm glad." Mom bent down and gave Mattie a hug.

When the hug ended, Mattie grabbed the snake, raced across the hall to Calvin's room, and tossed it inside. Noticing the look of relief on Mom's face, Mattie bounded happily down the stairs.

On the way to school, Mark practiced the spelling words for the test they'd be having that day. He wanted to make sure he did well on the test. "Camping. C-a-m-p-i-n-g. Camping."

"What about camping?" Mattie asked, trudging along beside him, looking like she was still half-asleep. "Are you hoping to go camping soon?"

"Nope." Mark kicked a pebble with the toe of his boot and sent it flying. "Camping is one of the words we'll have on our spelling test this morning."

Mattie groaned. "Oh, that's right, I forgot about the test."

"Does that mean you didn't study for it?" he asked.

"I studied a little bit."

"Just a little bit?"

Mattie nodded.

"Then don't expect to do well on the test."

"What are all the other words we'll be having?" Mattie asked. "I lost my list."

"If you didn't daydream so much you'd probably know where you put it."

"Are you gonna help me or not?" Mattie asked.

Looking down at his study sheet, Mark recited the words to his sister. "Camping, fishing, fuzzy, yesterday, zipper, dizzy, plastic, coolest, packed, vase, smell, grass, coming, summer, kitten, spins, bending, facts, think, and Sunday. Oh, and there's a bonus word—invention."

"Most of those words are hard—especially the bonus word." Mattie frowned. "I'll probably fail the test."

"You should have studied, Mattie."

"I was studying, but when you started teasing Twinkles with that rag, I went outside to ask you to stop, and I never got back to looking at the spelling words."

"Don't blame me for you not studying enough. If you fail the test you'll have no one to blame but yourself."

"Now you sound like Mom."

"I just think you need to study more so you'll get good grades. So let's practice some of these words while we walk."

"Okay."

Mark said a word, and then Mattie repeated it and tried spelling it correctly. She was doing pretty well until she spotted some yellow and white flowers growing along the edge of the road. "Oh, look at the pretty flowers. Wouldn't they look nice in our flower beds at home?"

Mark rolled his eyes. At least he'd offered to help

Mattie. If all she was going to think about was pretty flowers, she'd never pass her spelling test.

During noon recess that day, Mattie sat on the porch beside her friend Stella while they ate their lunches and visited.

"Are you still coming to my birthday supper next week?" Mattie asked, after she'd taken a bite of her peanut butter and jelly sandwich.

Stella bobbed her head. "I'm looking forward to it."

"Mark's invited your cousin, John, because as you know, he's Mark's best friend." Mattie smiled. "Oh, and my Grandpa and Grandma Miller will be there, too."

"What about your other grandparents—the ones who live in Burton?" Stella asked. "Won't they be at the birthday celebration, too?"

Mattie shook her head, feeling suddenly sad. "Grandpa Troyer's arthritis is acting up, so I don't think they'll be coming."

"That's too bad. I'm sure they'll send you both a gift, though."

"The best gift of all would be to see their smiling faces. That would make me so happy." Mattie took a drink of milk from her thermos. It was cold and refreshing.

"Get away from here!" someone hollered from across the porch.

Mattie turned to see what was going on, and was so surprised when she saw Twinkles with her little black nose inside Jared Herschberger's lunch pail, sniffing around. Mattie liked surprises, but not this kind, and she couldn't figure out what the dog was doing at the schoolhouse, but then she remembered that she'd forgotten to put Twinkles in her pen this morning.

"Go home, Twinkles!" Mattie shouted, clapping her hands. "Go home right now!"

Woof! Woof! Woof! Twinkles raced back and forth across the porch excitedly, stopping only to sniff several other children's lunch pails.

Mattie continued to holler at the dog, and so did some of the others, but Twinkles still wouldn't go. She wasn't being an obedient dog today, and Mattie was so embarrassed.

The teacher, Anna Ruth, stepped onto the porch just then and looked right at Mattie. "Is that your dog?"

Mattie nodded slowly, wishing at this moment that Twinkles belonged to someone else.

"Well, she can't be here at school. Please, take her home right now."

"Okay." Mattie didn't mind at all, because it would take her some time to walk home and back, which meant she'd miss taking the spelling test they'd be having soon.

"Oh, and since we'll be having the spelling test while you're gone, you'll have to stay after school to take it," Anna Ruth said.

Mattie frowned. It was bad enough that she hadn't studied much. Now she had to stay after school and take the spelling test. She realized her forgetfulness about not putting Twinkles away like Mom had told her to do this morning would probably get her in trouble with Mom, too. She wished she'd come down with a bad cold or the flu so she could have stayed home in bed today!

Chapter 11

Unexpected Gift

"What are you thinking about?" Mark asked, sneaking up behind Mattie and tickling the back of her neck with a feather.

She whirled around. "Absatz! You know I don't like to be tickled!"

"Aw, sure you do."

"No, I don't. Not when I'm thinking."

"What are you thinking about—the spelling test you failed at school last week?"

"Do you have to spoil our birthday by reminding me about that? Would you like me to keep reminding you about falling down the last time you tried to play baseball?"

"No, and I'm glad Anna Ruth has been letting me push some of the younger scholars on the swings during lunch recess, 'cause that's a lot more fun than playing baseball."

"I guess you are happier doing that," Mattie said, "but I'd rather play ball."

"That's because you're so good at it. It's always more

118

fun to do something you can do well than something you always mess up." Mark tickled Mattie's chin with the feather again. "So what were you thinking about when I snuck up on you?"

"I was wishing Grandma and Grandpa Troyer could be here for our birthday celebration tonight."

"I wish that, too. It would have been nice if Grandma had called and said Grandpa was feeling better by now. I've been praying for him."

"Same here," Mattie said with a nod.

Mark smiled. "Even though Grandma and Grandpa Troyer can't come for our party, when everyone else shows up I'm sure we'll have a good time."

"I hope so." Mattie's mouth turned up at the corners. "I'm glad our birthday's on a Saturday this year. I wouldn't have wanted to spend the day in school."

"Oh no, that would be baremlich." Mark snickered and slid the feather under Mattie's chin once more.

"Will you stop teasing?" She pushed his hand away. "If you don't, I'll find a feather and tickle you right back."

"You can't, because the only place I'm ticklish is on the bottom of my feet, and since I'm standing you can't tickle me there."

"If I was big like Dad or Ike, I'd pick you up and put you right on the ground," Mattie said. "Then I'd sit on you and tickle your feet till you couldn't stand it anymore."

Mark plopped his hands against his hips and crinkled his nose. "Well, you're not big like them, so don't even think about tickling my feet!"

Mattie flapped her hand at him, like she was shooing away a pesky fly. "Why don't you go play with your katze, or find someone else to tease with that feather?"

"Think I just might, 'cause you're so monotonous."

"Monotonous? What's that mean?" Mattie asked.

"It means you're boring." Mark gave Mattie one final tickle with the feather, and then he snickered all the way to the barn.

"Brothers," Mattie mumbled. "I wish today was just my birthday and not Mark's. Wonder what it'd be like to have a birthday all to myself and not have to share it with him?"

That evening Grandma and Grandpa Miller came for supper, along with Mattie's best friend, Stella, and Mark's best friend, John. There was enough food to feed a huge crowd. Mom fixed meat loaf, mashed potatoes, a tossed green salad, corn on the cob, and buttermilk biscuits. She even used their good dishes and put out the pretty stitched tablecloth with brightly colored squares on it, which made the birthday celebration even more festive.

"Umm. . .everything tastes appenditlich," Grandma said, smiling at Mom.

"Danki, I'm glad you think it's delicious," Mom said. "Mattie likes meat loaf and biscuits, and Mark likes mashed potatoes and corn on the cob, so I made both of their favorites."

"Who likes the tossed green salad?" Stella asked.

"I do," Mom said with a grin.

Mattie smiled, too. She appreciated the good supper Mom had made for her and Mark's birthday. She was glad their parents did nice things for them. She hoped that if she ever did become a parent when she grew up that she'd remember to do nice things for her children, too.

"What's for dessert?" Russell wanted to know.

"Homemade ice cream," Dad replied.

Mark's mouth drooped at the corners. "Do I have to crank the handle again? That's always hard work, and I don't think I should have to work hard on my birthday."

"No, you won't have to crank," Dad said with a chuckle. "Ike and I made the ice cream earlier, while you, Calvin, and Russell were doing your chores."

"What kind of ice cream is it?" Mark asked with a hopeful expression. He was probably hoping for chocolate this time.

"Vanilla, but your mamm has plenty of chocolate syrup for you to pour over the top."

"Are there strawberries, too?" Mattie questioned.

"Jah, I have plenty of strawberries." Mom patted Mattie's hand. "I also made you and Mark a birthday cake."

Mark smacked his lips. "Yum. Can we have our dessert as soon as we're done eating supper?"

"When I was your age I could eat a big meal and then gobble down my dessert right away," Grandpa Miller said. "But now that I'm older if I eat too much it goes right to my waist." He chuckled and thumped his stomach, while wiggling his bushy gray eyebrows. "So it's best if I wait and let my supper settle awhile before I eat anything more."

Stella looked over at Mattie and giggled. Mattie was glad her friend could be here to help celebrate her birthday. She hoped she'd be invited to Stella's for supper when her birthday came, because Stella was the best friend she'd ever had.

Mattie glanced over at Mark and frowned. He was licking the melted butter from his corn on the cob that had dripped onto his fingers. *Doesn't he have any manners at all?* she thought as she wiped her mouth and hands on a napkin.

"When can Mattie open the gift I brought her?" Stella asked, looking at Mom with a hopeful expression.

Mom smiled at Stella. "As soon as we're finished with supper we'll do up the dishes, eat our dessert, and then Mark and Mattie can open their presents."

"I can hardly wait for you to open my present," Stella whispered to Mattie. "I hope you'll like what I got you."

"Oh, I'm sure I will."

As they continued to eat their meal, the grownups talked about their gardens, farming, Dad's work in his woodshop, and also some things that had been going on in their community. Mattie had just finished her meat loaf, and was about to ask for another biscuit, when a knock sounded on the front door.

"Now I wonder who that could be? Our front door is seldom used by anyone except for strangers or some of our English neighbors," Dad said as he pushed back his chair and stood. "Guess I'd better go see who's come a-calling."

When Dad left the room, everyone resumed talking.

"Would you please pass me the basket of biscuits?" Mattie asked her brother Calvin. She could eat Mom's delicious homemade biscuits every day of the week.

Mark asked for another biscuit as well. As Mattie handed him the basket and then reached for the butter, Dad reentered the kitchen with a big grin on his face. A few seconds later, Grandma and Grandpa Troyer stepped into the room behind him.

Such commotion there was with Grandpa and Grandma's surprise arrival from Burton. Mark and Mattie squealed with delight; Mom shed a few tears, and there were lots of hugs and kisses going around.

Once the excitement calmed down, Dad added two more chairs to the table and Mom got out two more place settings. Grandma Troyer had even brought some of her delicious corn fritters, and also a pecan pie.

"We can't have a celebration without my fritters," Grandma said with a radiant smile. Corn fritters were Grandma's specialty, and the whole family was never disappointed whenever they went to Burton, because Grandma always made a big batch of tasty fritters.

Sitting around the table, everyone, especially the twins, wanted to hear all about how Grandpa Troyer was feeling.

"My arthritis has been doing better the last few days." Grandpa grinned as he stroked his bushy gray beard. "So this afternoon I looked at your grandma, and said, 'Let's hire a driver to take us to Walnut Creek, 'cause I don't think we should miss Mark and Mattie's birthday party.' " He looked across the table and winked at Mattie, and then Mark. "After all, it isn't every day that two of our grandchildren turn nine."

Mattie smiled, and so did Mark. "It's great to have you here," they said at the same time. Having Grandpa and Grandma Troyer here was a wonderful surprise!

Once supper was finished, Mom and both grandmas washed and dried the dishes, and the men headed outside to the porch to visit. Mattie and Stella went upstairs to play, while Mark took John out to the barn to see the kittens.

"Would you like to hold one of them?" Mark asked after he'd led John over to the box where Lucky's kittens were sleeping soundly.

John eagerly bobbed his blond head. "I kinda like the black one with four white paws."

"I call that one Boots," Mark said, gently picking up the kitten and placing it in John's lap. "That's the one I plan to keep."

John looked a bit disappointed at first, but then while stroking Boots's head, he smiled and said, "I figured Mattie and Stella would come out here, too."

"Nah. Mattie doesn't like cats, and I'm not sure about Stella." Mark took a seat on the bale of straw beside John.

"I can't imagine anyone not liking cats. Just listen to this little one purr," John said, looking down at Boots.

"Well, Mattie doesn't. But that's okay, 'cause I don't like her hund Twinkles either."

"How come?"

"That mutt's a real *pescht*. She's always underfoot and likes to nip at my leg."

"She's never nipped at me. Maybe she wants some attention and can somehow tell that you don't like her."

Mark nodded. "You're right about that, because I don't give her any attention."

"Maybe you should. You might learn to like the dog if you spent more time with her."

Just then Lucky leaped into Mark's lap. "You want a loyal pet, get a cat."

"I'd sure like one," John said. "Think I could have one of Lucky's busslin?"

"Don't see why not. She's got five of 'em, and Mom says we can only keep one, so that means we'll have to find homes for the other four." Mark motioned to the box, where the rest of the kittens lay curled up sleeping.

John smiled. "I'll ask my folks and see what they say. If they say jah, which one can I have?"

"Any but Boots." Mark pointed to a white kitten with black on the tip of its ears. "How about that one?"

John gave a nod. "That's fine with me. Think I'll call him 'Tippy.' "

The boys sat for a while, petting the cats. Then John said, "That sure was a surprise at supper when your other grandparents walked into the kitchen behind your dad."

"It sure was." Mark was glad God had answered his prayers about Grandpa Troyer. It was so good to have both sets of grandparents here to help them celebrate their special day. Mark knew he and Mattie weren't the only ones happy to see Grandpa and Grandma Troyer this evening. He'd seen the look of joy on Mom's face when she saw her parents enter the room. Her eyes had been filled with happy tears, and for a while she couldn't say a word. She'd jumped up and ran to her folks; then all three of them had hugged for a long time.

The boys continued to visit until Ike came out to the barn and told them that it was time to go into the house for cake and ice cream.

Mark put Lucky and Boots back in the box, and then he and John hurried toward the house. He was eager to eat some of that cold homemade ice cream and tasty cake.

When the boys entered the house, Mattie, Stella, and all the family were already gathered around the kitchen table. Mark and John took their seats, and then after Mom set the chocolate cake with vanilla icing on the table, everyone sang "Happy Birthday" to the twins. Next, Mom cut the cake and gave everyone a piece while Dad dished up the ice cream.

"Umm. . .this looks appenditlich," Mattie said as she spooned some strawberries on top of her ice cream.

"You're right, it is delicious," Mark said after he'd poured chocolate syrup over his, and taken a bite.

"This is really good, too." Grandma Troyer smiled as she ate a piece of cake.

"Danki." Mom reached over to pat her mother's hand. "Oh, we forgot to put your pecan pie on the table."

"Well, since we'll be spending the night, how about if we save the pie for tomorrow's dessert?" Grandma suggested. "Everyone seems to be enjoying the cake and ice cream, and that's probably more than enough."

"I think you're right about that," Mom agreed.

After Mark had gotten all the ice cream he could get with his spoon, he picked up the bowl and licked the rest of the ice cream out.

Mom frowned. "Don't be so rude, Mark. Where are your manners this evening?"

Mark's face heated. "Sorry, Mom. It just tasted so good I wanted to get every drop."

"Why don't we all go into the living room now, so Mark and Mattie can open their gifts?" Dad suggested after everyone had finished their cake and ice cream.

The twins didn't have to be asked twice. They hopped up from their chairs and scurried out of the kitchen.

When they'd all gathered in the living room, Mark and Mattie took seats on the sofa, while the others found places to sit, and Mom passed out the gifts.

The first present Mom handed Mattie was from Stella. Mattie tore the wrapping off the box, and seemed pleased to find a new baby doll inside.

"It's to replace the one Ada ruined," Stella whispered.

Mattie smiled and gave Stella a hug. "Danki. It's *wunderbaar*."

"I think it's wonderful, too," Mom said. "Since I wasn't able to get all the ink stains off your old doll's face, it's good that you have a new doll to replace it. Maybe we should give the ruined one to Ada to play with."

Mattie nodded and hugged the new doll to her chest.

After that, Mark opened the present John had brought him. It was a baseball mitt. Not so great for someone who didn't like to play ball, but he smiled and said, "Danki, John."

Next, Grandma and Grandpa Miller gave Mattie a drawing tablet and a box of colored pencils, and she seemed pleased. Mark got a new fishing pole, which he really liked.

"Danki," the twins told their grandparents.

Then, Grandma and Grandpa Troyer handed Mark and Mattie the gifts they had brought along for them.

"What's this?" Mark asked as he looked at the brightly painted clay pot that was inside the box he opened.

Grandpa Troyer laughed and winked at Mom as he explained that he'd heard about the frog Mark had put in the sugar bowl. "This is one of your grandma's old flower pots," he said. "As you can see there's a chunk of it missing around the top of the rim."

Mark gave a nod, although he didn't understand why they would give him such a strange gift, or what it had to do with the frog he'd put in the sugar bowl.

"One time when I was browsing around the garden center at our local hardware store," Grandpa went on to say, "I saw this cute little frog house they had for sale. You put it in a flower bed or around the bushes by the house, and apparently it attracts frogs. It's supposed to be a place for them to hide during the heat of the day." Grandpa continued by saying that when he caught Grandma getting ready to throw the old broken pot away, he'd looked it over real good, turned it upside down, and realized it could be used as a frog house. "The missing chunk on the rim of the flower pot makes

a perfect doorway for a frog, or even a toad to enter."
Grandpa grinned widely. "So with some paint to touch
it up, Grandma and I decided that it would make the
perfect gift for you, Mark—especially after hearing
about your little frog incident."

Everyone agreed it was a unique and appropriate gift.
Mark said he really liked it, and thanked them both.

Then Grandma Troyer handed Mattie her gift. It
was a beautiful pot of bright yellow mums. "There's no
better way to feel close to God than to find a lovely spot
in the yard that you can call your own and plant some
flowers He's created for our enjoyment," she said, giving
Mattie a hug.

"Danki, Grandma." Knowing how much Mom
enjoyed tending the flowers in her garden, Mark figured
Mattie would have fun finding her own little spot to dig
in the dirt, too.

"Remember now, Mattie," Grandpa Troyer said,
"don't tell anyone else about your mums."

"How come?" Mattie questioned. The rest of the
family seemed to be waiting for his answer as well.

With a twinkle in his eyes, Grandpa Troyer
announced, "Well, because 'mum's the word!' "

Mattie giggled. "Oh Grandpa, now I know where
Mark gets his teasing from."

They all had a good laugh about that.

"Okay, now, Mark and Mattie, it's our turn." Dad
motioned to the door. "Your mother's and my gift is
waiting for you outside, so let's all go out there and see
how you like it."

Everyone hurried out the door, and when they stepped onto the porch Dad pointed to a strange-looking bicycle in the yard. It was bigger than any bike Mark had ever seen, and it had two seats, two handlebars, and two sets of pedals.

Mark looked at Mattie, and she looked at him; then they both looked at Mom and Dad. "What's that?" they asked at the same time.

"It's a bicycle built for two." Mom smiled widely. "It's a secondhand bike that we saw advertised in the local newspaper for a reasonable price. Since we couldn't afford to get two new bikes, we decided to get one bike that you could ride together."

Mark couldn't think of a thing to say. Mattie didn't say anything either. They just stood there staring at the unexpected gift with their mouths hanging open.

"Hop on and try it out," Grandpa Miller said. "It should be a lot of fun."

Mark sat on the front seat. Mattie took the back. Mark pedaled. Mattie just sat there.

"You both have to pedal," Grandpa Troyer said.

Mark pedaled. Mattie pedaled. The bike swerved to the left, then to the right. They pedaled and weaved back and forth some more, until the bike toppled over. The twins fell on the ground with a thud.

"Are either of you hurt?" Mom asked with a worried expression.

"I'm fine, but that sure wasn't fun," Mattie mumbled, picking herself up.

"I'm okay, too." Mark kicked at a stone beneath his

feet. "Think I'd rather ride the bike by myself."

"It just takes practice," Mom said. "Put your heads together and figure it out."

"That's right," Dad agreed. "You need to think alike and work together to make the bike go. Just remember, two heads are better than one."

Chapter 12

Mattie's Decision

For the next week, Mark and Mattie practiced riding their new bicycle, but they couldn't seem to work together so the bike wouldn't wobble all over the place, and it either went too fast or too slow. When Mark rode up front, Mattie didn't pedal hard enough and he had to do all the work. When Mattie rode up front, she didn't steer right and the bike vibrated and went crooked. The other day when they'd ridden their bike to school, Mattie had been up front, and she'd pedaled so fast that Mark's hat flew off his head. Even some of the flowers Mattie had attached to the basket at the front of the bike had blown off. Mattie was a reckless, crazy driver; that was for sure!

"I don't like the bicycle built for two," Mark told Mattie one Saturday morning, after breakfast. "Mom said we should keep practicing, but I'm not going to ride it today."

"That's fine with me," Mattie said with a nod. "Anyway, I'd rather do something fun, and riding that silly bike sure isn't fun."

"Think I'll go out to the barn and play with Lucky's busslin. Want to come?" Mark asked.

She shook her head. "No thanks. I have better things to do than get my hands all scratched up by those frisky little kittens."

"Aw, it doesn't hurt that much," Mark said. "You just need to know how to handle them."

"I don't want to handle them, 'cause I don't like katze. Think I'll go find Twinkles." Mattie hurried away.

Mark shrugged and headed for the barn. If Mattie preferred to play with her irritating dog instead of petting the cuddly kittens, that was fine with him.

When Mark stepped inside the barn, he nearly bumped into Calvin.

"Russell and I are goin' fishing again." Calvin motioned to the fishing pole he held. "Wanna come?"

Mark shook his head. "Not today. Think I'm gonna play with the busslin awhile, and then I may read a buch."

Calvin shrugged his shoulders. "If you'd rather read a book than go fishing that's up to you, but I thought you'd wanna try out that new fishing pole Grandpa gave you. I'm sure Grandpa's eager to hear how you like it."

"Some other time," Mark said. "I don't really feel like fishin' today."

"Suit yourself, brainiac."

Mark frowned. "It's bad enough that some of the kids at school call me that; I don't need you saying it, too."

Calvin ruffled Mark's hair. "Don't get yourself all worked up; I was only teasing. The kids who call you brainiac are probably jealous because studying comes easy to you, and you get better grades than they do."

"They could get good grades, too, if they studied more," Mark said. "I tell that to Mattie all the time, but she thinks she doesn't do well because she's dumm."

"She wouldn't think so if she studied harder instead of daydreaming all the time."

Mark nodded. "I agree."

"Well, guess I'd better see if Russell's ready to go. We'll be at the Raber's Pond if you change your mind about fishing." Calvin gave Mark's shoulder a squeeze and hurried out the door.

Mark went over to the box where the kittens were kept and found them all sleeping. He didn't want to disturb them so he left the barn and went up to his room to get a book. Then he went back outside and flopped on the grass, listening to the cicadas singing noisily in the trees. With the cool weather that was just around the corner, Mark knew he wouldn't be hearing the annual cicada much longer. But for now, like all summer long, he'd enjoy the noisy insects as they sang their loud buzzing song from sunup to sunset. At night, when the cicadas quieted, the katydids and crickets took over. It seemed there was always some sort of bug sound during the summer and early fall months. Since they were back in school again, it was nice to have a lazy day like this when he could read or just watch the clouds as they drifted across the sky.

Mark stayed there awhile; then he decided to try to look for a place to put his new frog house. As he walked around the yard looking for just the right spot, he noticed a praying mantis perched on a branch in one of Mom's azalea bushes.

He stepped up for a closer look and watched in amazement as the sneaky praying mantis moved in very slowly on an unsuspecting multicolored ladybug.

"Leave that cute little bug alone and pick on someone your own size," Mark said, scooping the ladybug into his hand. He smiled when he set it free. "Besides, ladybugs are supposed to bring good luck."

Of course, Mark knew that was only a superstition, but he still wanted to save the little ladybug.

The praying mantis turned its head toward Mark, as if to say, "Hey, that was my lunch you just stole."

Just then Mark spotted a grasshopper leaping through the flower bed below. *Zip!*—he reached down and caught it on the first try. Then, knowing the praying mantis needed something to eat, Mark set the grasshopper on the azalea bush. It didn't take long for the praying mantis to turn its head and spot its next meal. Then it slowly approached the grasshopper, rose up right over it, wobbled a bit, and just that quick, it snatched the bug in its forelegs. Immediately, the mantis started chomping on its prey.

Mark knew if Mattie had seen that she'd probably say, "Eww. . .", but he thought it was kind of neat. After all, the praying mantis needed something to eat.

Thinking about Mattie, he remembered seeing her on the porch swing when he'd gone out to the barn earlier. He glanced toward the house and saw that she was still there. Maybe after he'd watched the praying mantis awhile longer he'd go have a little talk with Mattie, because there was a question he wanted to ask her.

Mattie pushed her feet against the wooden floorboards to get the porch swing moving faster. It was nice to just sit and listen to the cicadas and birds, while she rocked back and forth and admired the pretty yellow mums Grandpa and Grandma Troyer had given her. Yesterday afternoon, Mom had helped Mattie prepare one corner of the flower bed that she could call her own. That's where Mattie planted the mum, and she had plans to plant a few other flowers there as well. Dad had even been nice enough to make Mattie a little wooden sign that said MATTIE'S CORNER. It was fun to have her own place in the yard that she didn't have to share with anyone.

Purr. . . Purr. . . Purr. . .

Mattie looked to the left and saw Lucky lying on the window ledge with her nose resting between her paws.

Mattie muttered, "You oughta be in the barn taking care of your busslin instead of out here sleeping."

Lucky just ignored her and kept sleeping and purring.

Mattie looked away from Mark's cat and glanced into the yard. There lay Twinkles on top of the picnic table. Silly dog liked to sleep in strange places. One time a few weeks ago, Mattie had discovered Twinkles on the roof of their house, sound asleep. Another time she'd found the dog sleeping on the front seat of Dad's buggy. Dad hadn't been happy about that at all, because

Twinkles had left some of her dog hair behind, which meant Dad had to clean the seat before they could take the horse and buggy to church that Sunday.

Bzzz. . . Bzzz. . . Bzzz. . . Mattie looked up and saw a fly circling her head. "Go on now—shoo." She swatted at the pesky insect, thankful that it wasn't a bee. The fly finally flew off the porch and into the yard.

Mattie closed her eyes and leaned her head against the back of the swing, as she focused on the birds in their yard, singing a sweet melody. There were still a few songbirds left, but this time of the year a lot of them had started migrating south. In a few more weeks the squawking blue jays and the crows with their *caw, caw, caw* sound would be some of the few birds serenading everyone until spring arrived again the following year.

Bzzz. . . Bzzz. . . Bzzz. . . There was that pesky fly again.

Mattie, with her eyes still closed, reached up and swatted at the sound of the insect.

"Ouch!" A terrible stinging sensation shot through her finger, and Mattie's eyes popped open. She gasped when she saw a bumblebee sitting on her finger, even after the sting. She flicked it away and winced as she pulled out the stinger. So now she knew what it felt like to be stung by a bee. Just like everyone had said, it really smarted. Well, she didn't like it one little bit and hoped it never happened to her again!

Woof! Woof! Twinkles bounded onto the porch. *Woof! Woof! Woof!* She jumped up to the window ledge and nipped at Lucky's fluffy tail.

Meow! The cat leaped into the air and landed on the lounge chair below the window, catching her feet in the webbing. Poor Lucky just lay there all flattened out.

Even though Mattie didn't care much for Mark's cat, she couldn't let the poor critter stay like that. So she bent down, carefully untangled the cat's feet, and picked her up.

Lucky growled and sank her claws into Mattie's arm.

"Yeow!" Mattie dropped the cat on the porch. "So that's the thanks I get for trying to help you," she muttered. "Maybe I should have left you stuck there in that chair!"

Woof! Woof! Twinkles chased after Lucky as she leaped off the porch. Round and round the yard they went, with Twinkles barking frantically, and Lucky screeching like her tail was on fire.

"What's going on?" Mark called, as he raced around the house and into the backyard.

Mattie quickly explained all that had happened. "Just look what Lucky did to me." She showed Mark the painful scratches on her arm. "Now thanks to her I'm miserable."

He frowned. "I'm sorry she scratched you, but it wouldn't have happened if your hund hadn't nipped at my cat's tail. You oughta keep Twinkles locked up in her pen."

Mattie shook her head. "That wouldn't be fair. Lucky should have been in the barn with her busslin instead of sleeping on the window ledge."

"She can't be in the barn every single minute. She

needs some time to herself," Mark said. "Besides, all the busslin are sleeping right now."

Mattie held her finger out to Mark. "Not only did your cat scratch me, but I got a bee sting."

"When did that happen?" he asked.

"Right before Twinkles scared Lucky."

"Does it hurt much?" Mark really did look concerned.

"Jah, but the stinger came right out."

Mark touched Mattie's arm. "I'm sorry that happened."

"Me, too, but I guess everyone gets a bee sting sometime in their life." Mattie stepped off the porch.

"Where are you going?" he called.

"Out to the garden to check on my pretty mums and see if they need any water."

"Say, Mattie, there's something else I want to say," Mark said, tagging along beside her.

"What's that?"

"It's about your little flower bed."

Mattie stopped walking and tipped her head. "What about it?"

"Well, I was wondering if I could put my frog house in your garden."

"Why would you want to put it there? You have the whole yard to choose a spot for the old flower pot Grandma and Grandpa Troyer gave you."

"It's not just an old pot," Mark said. "It's a frog house. Or at least it will be once a frog finds the clay pot and makes it his home."

Mattie shrugged her shoulders. "So that doesn't answer my question. Why would you want to put it in my flower garden?"

Mark's face turned pink. "I just thought. . . Well, that yellow mum Grandma and Grandpa gave you is awful pretty, and maybe some frog will think so, too, and it'll hop right into your little garden. Then when it sees the clay pot, it'll hop inside."

Mattie tapped her chin as she gave Mark's request some serious thought. The nice flower bed with the beautiful yellow mums was supposed to be her space and no one else's, so she had a decision to make. Should she let Mark put his frog house there, or tell him to find another spot?

CHAPTER 13

Mud Bath

"I don't see why we can't walk to school today," Mattie grumbled as she and Mark took their bicycle out of the barn the following Friday morning.

"Mom says we need to practice," he replied. "Besides, we can get there quicker riding than walking."

"Well, if we have to go to school on the bike, then I want to ride up front."

"You rode up front the last time, and you drove so *narrisch* the bike almost fell over," Mark reminded.

Mattie shook her head. "I didn't drive crazy."

"Jah, you did. You were swerving all over the place, just like a crooked snake."

"I was not."

"Were, too."

"Was not."

Mark pointed to the back of the bicycle. "Just get on and don't be so divergent."

Mattie put her hands against her hips and frowned. "Would you please stop using words I don't know?"

"Divergent means 'contrary,' " Mark said.

"I'm not contrary. I just don't think you should get your way all the time. If you'll remember, I let you put your frog house in my garden, but I don't see why I have to do everything you ask."

"Fine then. We'll go back in the house and talk to Mom about this."

Mattie knew if they did that, Mom would tell them to stop arguing, work it out, and get to school. She also knew if they didn't leave now they'd be late. So reluctantly she climbed onto the back of the bike while Mark took his seat at the front.

As they rode along the trail near the road, Mattie didn't say much. Instead, she focused on the leaves on the trees that were beginning to slowly change color. It wouldn't be long before they fell off the trees, and then Mattie and Mark could play in the leaves they would pile up after raking them first.

Mattie sniffed the air. It was crisp—like the spicy scent of pine. She also noticed it was the first morning she could see her breath in the air. Apple-picking time was just around the corner, and then Dad would make sweet cider using the apples from the tree in their backyard. Mattie's mouth watered. She could almost taste the juicy liquid trickling down her throat.

"What are you doing back there?" Mark hollered over his shoulder. "You're not pedaling, and you can't expect me to do all the work up here."

"I am so pedaling!"

"No, you're not."

Mattie started pedaling real hard—so hard that her

legs began to ache. "There, is that fast enough for you?"

"Now you're pedaling too hard!" Mark shouted. "I can't steer right if we're going too fast."

The bike wobbled, and Mattie screamed. She was sure she was going to fall off.

Mark kept going until Mattie quit pedaling. When they started up a hill, he had to stop. That was when Mattie hopped off.

"What are you doing? Why aren't you helping me pedal?"

"I'm not going to ride this bike anymore. I'm walking the rest of the way to school."

Mattie grabbed her schoolbooks from the basket and hurried off. She could hear Mark huffing and puffing behind her as he pedaled by himself.

Mark gripped the handlebars as he tried to pedal the bike alone. It wasn't easy without Mattie, and he wished she was still behind him helping right now. But no, she'd taken the shortcut to school through the Hostetlers's cornfield, leaving Mark to fend for himself.

Mark huffed and puffed awhile longer and finally got off the bike, pushing it the rest of the way to school. He'd just entered the schoolyard when the teacher rang the bell, so he quickly parked the bike and hurried up the porch steps, taking them two at a time. When he entered the schoolhouse, he saw Mattie putting her jacket and lunch pail away. He was tempted to say something to her, but he didn't want to talk about it in front of the other scholars. So he put his lunch pail away, hung his straw hat on a wall peg, and took a seat at his desk.

Their teacher began the day as usual, by reading several verses of scripture from the Bible to the class, and then after the Lord's Prayer had been said, everyone filed to the front of the room to sing a few songs. Next, grades three to eight were given their arithmetic assignments, which the teacher wrote on the blackboard. While they worked on that, the first and second graders had a lesson in phonics.

Mark listened to Anna Ruth help one of the younger girls for a while; then he watched a second-grade boy use his fingers to count.

He finally pulled his gaze away from the boy, knowing he needed to get busy doing the work on his desk. He wasn't as good at arithmetic as he was spelling, but by studying hard and not daydreaming like Mattie always did he usually managed to do well on most of his arithmetic tests.

Before Anna Ruth dismissed the class for lunch at noon, the scholars lined up by the sink to wash their hands. Ordinarily, most of the scholars ate their lunches outside, but since it had started to rain a short time ago, everyone ate at their desks today. Afterward, they played some indoor games, which Mark thought was great.

By the time school was over, it was raining so hard that huge puddles had formed all over the ground. After the way Mattie had acted earlier, Mark figured he'd be stuck riding the bike home by himself, but he was surprised when she climbed onto the back and said, "Let's hurry home so we don't get too wet!"

Mark and Mattie did fairly well as they pedaled up the first hill, but when they started down the other side, they were moving too fast, and it was hard to control the bike.

"Use your brake, Mattie. Use your brake!" Mark shouted.

"I am!" she hollered.

"No, you're not! We're going way too fast!"

The bike slowed some, but then it started to wobble. Mark gripped the handlebars tightly and gritted his teeth. In his determination to get control of the bike, he wasn't watching where they were going. The next thing he knew, they'd ridden into the middle of a huge mud puddle. Water sprayed in every direction, soaking their feet.

"I'm getting wet!" Mattie screamed in Mark's ear.

"I know. . .me, too!"

Suddenly, the bike tipped to the right; then it wobbled to the left. Mark slipped off, and Mattie fell, too. They landed in the murkiest part of the puddle!

Mattie clambered to her feet and stared down at her dress with a scowl. "Ugh! I'm a mess!"

Suddenly, Mattie's frown turned upside down, and she stared to laugh as she pointed at the muddy water dripping off Mark's hat and onto his nose. "It looks like we both took a mud bath," she said.

Mark chuckled, too. "Jah, we sure did!"

CHAPTER 14

Teamwork

The following Saturday, after Mattie helped Mom cut up apples for the pies she planned to bake, she cleaned her room, and then carried a bucket of water across the yard to give Twinkles. She was almost to the dog pen when—*smack!*—a bright red apple hit her arm. Water splashed out of the bucket, soaking Mattie's dress.

"Hey!" She whirled around and saw Mark near the apple tree.

"Sorry," Mark said. "I was tossing the rotten apples into the field for the cows, and didn't expect anyone to get in the way. Guess I should've been watchin' closer."

"Well, please be more careful from now on. Maybe you should put all the rotten apples in the wheelbarrow and push it next to the fence. Then you can drop the apples into the field for the cows."

Mark smiled. "Good idea!"

As Mark headed for the barn to get the wheelbarrow, Mattie hurried to the dog pen. She'd just finished giving Twinkles some water when Mom stepped onto the porch and called for her to come.

When Mattie entered the house a few minutes later, she found Mom lying on the sofa with a wet washcloth over her eyes.

"What's wrong, Mom?" Mattie asked. "Are you grank?"

Mom removed the washcloth, and a large crease formed across her forehead as she squinted. "I'm not sick, but I do have a *koppweh*."

"I'm sorry you have a headache. Do you need me to do anything for you?"

Mom nodded slowly. "I was hoping you and Mark could ride over to the store in Walnut Creek and get me some aspirin."

"On our bicycle built for two?"

"Jah. That would be much faster than walking."

After the way things had gone all week with her and Mark and their bicycle built for two, Mattie didn't want to go anywhere with him. But she knew Mom needed the aspirin for her headache, so she smiled and said, "Okay, we'll go."

Mark's legs ached as he and Mattie left the store. He'd done most of the pedaling on the way there, because Mattie kept forgetting to pedal and wanted to talk about the pretty colored leaves scattered along the edge of the road and the birds singing in the trees overhead. Mark hoped their ride home would go better, but figured Mattie probably wouldn't cooperate then, either.

On the way back from Walnut Creek, they rode in silence for a while, and then as they neared the schoolhouse, Mattie stopped pedaling.

"Keep your legs moving," Mark said. "We'll never get home if you don't help me pedal."

"I see some of our friends are over there playing ball," she said excitedly. "Let's stop and say hello."

"Huh-uh."

"Why not?"

"They might want us to play ball, and we don't have time for that. We've got to get the aspirin home to Mom, remember?" Truth was, that wasn't the only reason Mark didn't want to stop. He was worried that he might get stuck playing ball, and then if he did something dumb and messed up, everyone would make fun of him.

Mattie tapped Mark on the shoulder. "I just want to stop a few minutes so I can talk to Stella."

"Okay, but I'm not going to play ball." Mark stopped the bicycle near the ball field, and they both got off. While Mark parked the bike, Mattie raced over to Stella, who stood off to the side with some other girls, watching the game. Mark leaned on the wooden fence and watched his friend John, who was up to bat. He was glad no one had pushed the issue of him playing ball today. He got tired of the other boys making fun of him. His failure at playing the game well gave the guys more reason to call him names. He tried hard to hide it, but the nicknames really did hurt his feelings.

Mark had to admit, Mattie always came to his rescue, although that embarrassed him, too. She'd been teased a time or two about her red hair as well, but it didn't seem to bother her, so the other kids didn't waste their time taunting Mattie anymore. And they backed off quickly when she stood up for Mark, but he still wished she wouldn't defend him.

The ball whizzed out of the pitcher's hand and went straight over home plate, pulling Mark's thoughts aside.

"Strike one!" Allen Hostetler shouted from where he stood behind John.

Another ball left the pitcher's hand, coming fast and hard, and it was heading straight toward John.

"Look out!" Mark hollered, but it was too late. The ball hit the side of John's head, knocking him to the ground.

John lay there, unmoving.

"Oh no! Is he dead?" someone shouted. Then everyone ran over to John and started talking at once.

"I think he's hurt bad."

"I see blood on his head."

"Is he breathing?"

"Jah. Look there. His chest is moving."

"We need to get help," Allen said, his dark eyes wide with fear. "Where's the nearest phone shack so we can call 911?"

"Mattie and Mark's house is the closest," Stella spoke up. She looked at Mattie and then Mark. "Will you two go for help?"

Mark didn't hesitate to nod. His best friend had been hurt, and he wanted to get help for him right away. "Come on, Mattie!" he shouted. "Let's get on our bicycle and ride like the wind. We've got to get help for John!"

Without any quarreling, Mattie climbed onto the

back of the bike, and Mark took his seat at the front, whispering a prayer for his friend. Then off they went down the road. Mark didn't have to remind Mattie to pedal this time, and they both kept the bike moving steady. No more wobbling or driving like a crooked snake. It was the first time they'd ridden the bicycle built for two without arguing, and they did everything just right. Maybe this bike wasn't so bad after all. Maybe, despite their differences, they could do something together.

"I'm sure worried about John," Mark called over his shoulder, his heart beating hard in his chest. "What if he's hurt really bad? What if. . ."

"He's gonna be okay," Mattie said, letting go of the handlebar with one hand, and patting Mark's shoulder. "We'll be home soon, and then we can go to our phone shack and call for help. We just need to pray and hope for the best."

"You're right." Mark felt a little better now. Hearing his sister's calm voice and her reassuring words gave him the faith to believe that God would answer his prayers.

As Mark and Mattie continued to pedal in unison, they even conquered the hills, which at any other time they'd have ended up walking the bike up.

In no time at all their house came into view. They stopped the bike in front of the phone shack, and Mark called 911 while Mattie ran up to the house to give Mom the bottle of aspirin and tell her what had happened.

❖

"I heard what happened at the schoolhouse with your friend John today," Dad said as Mattie and Mark sat at the table eating supper with their family that evening. "It's good you and Mattie were there and rode home so quickly to call for help."

"It was the first time we rode our bicycle as a team," Mark said.

"That's right," Mattie agreed. "Before we didn't like riding the bike, but today we didn't even think about that. We just pedaled hard and rode straight home." She smiled at Mark. "It was like we were a team. And now I kinda like having a bike that's different from everyone else's."

He grinned back at her. "You're right, and I agree."

"It just goes to show that even though each of you likes different things, you can do something together and do it well," Mom put in.

The twins both nodded. Mattie was glad Mom was feeling better. After she'd taken an aspirin and rested awhile this afternoon, she'd been her own smiling self again.

"It's just like Grandpa Miller told us once," Mattie said. "Mark and I are both special. In fact, there's no one just like either of us. We're unequalled—we're unique."

"You've got that right," Russell said with a snicker. He bumped Mark's arm with his elbow. "I've never met anyone who likes to tease and play tricks on other people the way you do."

"And don't forget about our sister Mattie. She's different, too." Ike winked at Mattie. "I've never met anyone who likes to decorate so many things with flowers—even the fence posts."

Mattie's cheeks warmed. "I just like our yard to look pretty."

"There's nothing wrong with that." Dad reached in front of Mark to get the saltshaker.

"You two sure haven't eaten much." Mom motioned to Mark's plate, and then to Mattie's. "Aren't you hungerich this evening? Don't you like my savory stew?"

"I like it fine, Mom," Mattie said. "I'm just not all that hungry right now."

Mark bobbed his head. "Same goes for me. I can't think about food 'cause I'm worried about John. Sure wish we'd hear something about how he's doing."

"It's probably taking some time for him to be examined," Dad said. "And the doctor's most likely running some tests."

"Are they gonna make John take a test even when he's not at school?" Mattie's eyes widened.

Russell chuckled. "No, silly. The doctor will run some tests on John to see how badly he's injured. Isn't that right, Dad?"

Dad nodded. "I'm sure we'll hear something soon."

A few minutes later, there was a knock on the back door.

"I'll get it," Ike said, pushing away from the table. He hurried from the kitchen, and when he returned, John's older brother, Peter, was with him.

"Just came by to tell you that John has a slight concussion and a nasty bruise on his head, but he's going to be okay." Peter smiled at the twins. "I heard how you two went for help when my bruder got hurt today. Danki for being such good friends."

"We were glad we could get home so quickly," Mark said.

"Jah," Mattie agreed. "And since we rode our bicycle built for two, we got here really fast."

Peter's smile widened. "My family is very grateful, because thanks to you, John got the help he needed, and quite promptly, too."

"Tell John that I'll be over to see him soon after he gets home from the hospital," Mark said. "Oh, and I'll bring the kitten he wanted, too. That should help him feel better."

"That's real nice of you," Peter said. "My bruder's lucky to have a good friend like you."

"I'm lucky to have John for a friend, too."

After Peter left, Dad put one hand on Mark's shoulder and one hand on Mattie's. "We all appreciate you, and we're pleased that you not only acted quickly on John's behalf today, but you have finally learned how to work together as a team." He gave their shoulders a gentle pat. "You two are quite a pair!"

About the Author

Wanda E. Brunstetter is a bestselling author who enjoys writing historical, as well as Amish-themed novels. Descended from Anabaptists herself, Wanda became fascinated with the Plain People when she married her husband, Richard, who grew up in a Mennonite church in Pennsylvania. Wanda and her husband live in Washington State. They have two grown children and six grandchildren. Wanda and Richard often travel the country, visiting their many Amish friends and gathering further information about the Amish way of life. In her spare time, Wanda enjoys photography, ventriloquism, gardening, reading, stamping, and having fun with her family. Visit Wanda's Website at www.wandabrunstetter.com and feel free to e-mail her at wanda@wandabrunstetter.com.

Rachel Yoder— Always Trouble Somewhere!

Join Rachel Yoder on a series of adventures with these 4-in-1 story collections written by bestselling author of Amish fiction Wanda E. Brunstetter. Whether Rachel is bringing frogs to church, chasing ornery roosters, or taking wild buggy rides, girls will encounter a lovable character who finds trouble nipping at her bare-footed heels at every turn!

Look Out, Lancaster County!

Growing Up in Lancaster County

Available wherever books are sold.

Find Mattie and Mark
Online!

Visit Amish Fiction for Kids online for:

Games
Puzzles
Vocabulary Words
& Much More!

www.AmishFictionForKids.com